Résistance: Contes de la Seconde Guerre mondiale en France

Édith Thomas and her nephews, Daniel Thomas and Jacques Thomas. Photograph by Madeleine Thomas. Used with permission of Daniel Thomas and Jacques Thomas.

ÉDITH THOMAS

Résistance: Contes de la Seconde Guerre mondiale en France

Edited by

Michelle Chilcoat

Introduction by

Michelle Chilcoat and Lori J. Marso

Foreword by

Dorothy Kaufmann

Modern Language Association of America

New York 2022

Library of Congress Cataloging-in-Publication Data
Names: Thomas, Édith, author. | Chilcoat, Michelle, editor, writer of introduction. | Marso, Lori Jo, writer of introduction. | Kaufmann, Dorothy, writer of foreword.
Title: Résistance : contes de la Seconde Guerre Mondiale en France / Édith Thomas ; edited by Michelle Chilcoat ; introduction by Michelle Chilcoat and Lori J. Marso ; foreword by Dorothy Kaufmann. Other titles: Contes d'Auxois
Description: New York : Modern Language Association of America, 2022. | Series: Texts and translations, 1079-252X ; 34 | Includes bibliographical references. | Summary: "A collection of short stories by Édith Thomas (1909–70), first published as Contes d'Auxois. Portrays resistance by ordinary people during the Nazi occupation of Vichy France in World War II. Explores the nature of heroism, the identity of one's allies and enemies, and the ways individuals can find solidarity"— Provided by publisher.
Identifiers: LCCN 2021021182 (print) | LCCN 2021021183 (ebook) | ISBN 9781603294997 (paperback) | ISBN 9781603295000 (EPUB)
Subjects: LCSH: World War, 1939–1945—France—Fiction. | France—History—German occupation, 1940–1945—Fiction. | LCGFT: Short stories.
Classification: LCC PQ2639.H56 C6 2022 (print) | LCC PQ2639.H56 (ebook) | DDC 843/.912—dc23
LC record available at https://lccn.loc.gov/2021021182
LC ebook record available at https://lccn.loc.gov/2021021183

Texts and Translations 34

ISSN 1079-252x

Cover illustration: *Honneur au Maquis.* c. 1941. Mary Evans Picture Library / Grenville Collins Postcard Collection.

Published by The Modern Language Association of America
85 Broad Street, Suite 500, New York, New York 10004-2434
www.mla.org

Édith Thomas. *Contes d'Auxois.* Les Éditions de Minuit, 1943. Reprinted by permission of Daniel Thomas.

Contents

Foreword: Writing Underground

Dorothy Kaufmann

Édith Thomas played a crucial role in what the French call *la Résistance intellectuelle*, the struggle to counter Nazi and Vichy propaganda by giving voice to forbidden discourse. She was the lone woman in the Paris network of French Resistance writers and contributed her *Contes d'Auxois*, published here as *Stories of Resistance*, as well as articles and poems, to the underground press. Michelle Chilcoat's excellent translation revives these stories for English-speaking readers, and as Chilcoat and Lori Marso emphasize in their informative introduction, *Contes d'Auxois* contains tales of "everyday acts of resistance," in which ordinary French women and men—and even a German soldier—say no to the occupying Nazi forces.

After the trauma of France's collapse and occupation by Nazi Germany, the majority of French people chose neither resistance nor active collaboration but various forms of accommodation with the Germans. Resistance was the response of a small minority. Thomas's immediate response to the occupation is a harbinger of that resistance. On 25 June 1940, the day the armistice with Germany took effect, Thomas writes in her diary: "On va nous apprendre désormais à haïr tout ce que nous avions aimé et ce que nous avions raison d'aimer. On va désormais nous apprendre que c'est la raison qui a tort et la folie et le désespoir qui sont la plus grande sagesse" (*Pages* 77). She goes on to warn her compatriots of what lies ahead: "des cimetières et des camps de concentration, l'ordre moral des morts" (78). A few weeks later, she asks herself: "Que peut-on *faire*?" (88). What she could do was serve the Resistance by writing.

Writing for the underground press, like every other kind of resistance, was dangerous; censorship laws severely restricted the information that could be released and the themes that could be developed in publications. A series of regulations pertaining to the production and distribution of undesirable publications reinforced the censorship laws. Another law stipulated that anyone who received anti-German tracts had to inform the local Kommandantur, or military headquarters. Persons who helped distribute tracts were warned that they would be among the first hostages.

In October 1940 Raymond Deiss, a cousin of Thomas's father, began printing and distributing the first underground publication of the occupation, *Pantagruel*, named after the irreverent Renaissance hero in François Rabelais's novel *Gargantua and Pantagruel*. Each issue of *Pantagruel* appeared in linotype on two double sheets that were clearly and elegantly typed. In 1941 Deiss was arrested, along with his two associates. None of them survived. Deiss was sent to prison in Cologne, Germany, and later was decapitated with an ax. The modest aim of his journal had been "le maintien de notre droit millénaire à penser par nous-mêmes" (qtd. in Bellanger 34).

In 1942 Thomas began writing for the underground publication *Les lettres françaises*, which at the time consisted of a few sheets reproduced on a mimeograph. Thomas headlined her first article in large, bold calligraphic letters, "Crier la vérité!"[1] In the article she speaks about what she has witnessed: "les étoiles sur les poitrines, l'arrachement des enfants aux mères, les hommes qu'on fusille chaque jour, la dégradation méthodique de tout un peuple" (1). The article was a call to writers to be faithful to their vocation, which meant crying out the truth of what they saw happening around them.

Thomas's *Contes d'Auxois* was published in 1943 by Les Éditions de Minuit, an astonishing underground publishing house that had no equivalent anywhere in occupied Europe. The purpose of Les Éditions de Minuit was twofold: to make it possible for French writers to be published in France without having to submit to censorship, and, just as important, to project to the world an image of France that would counter the image projected by the Vichy government. Although a clandestine publishing house would seem to be an oxymoron, Pierre de Lescure and Jean Bruller, the founders of Les Éditions de Minuit, were determined to produce a series of volumes free of any concession to the enemy, books that would show real literary value and demonstrate to the world that the French spirit was still alive. In a further act of defiance, the presentation of each book was aesthetically of high quality, from the paper and the typography to the book's binding. All the difficulties of production and distribution confronted by underground tracts and newspapers were compounded in this far more ambitious enterprise; there was also the problem of finding authors willing to publish books under conditions that not only were dangerous but also required anonymity.

Yvonne Paraf, the woman who bound books for the publisher in her home, had the idea of designating Les Éditions de Minuit authors by the regions of France with which they felt a special connection. Most of the stories in *Contes d'Auxois*, taken from real events, are set in or around Sainte-Aulde, a village on the Marne River where Thomas's mother lived in the family home. Thomas may have adapted her pseudonym, Auxois, from the name of a neighboring village, Orxois.

The change in the note at the back of each volume published by Les Éditions de Minuit is revealing. In volumes published before 1943, the note reads: "Ce volume publié aux dépens d'un patriote a été achevé d'imprimer sous l'occupation nazie" (Vercors)—and ends with the publication date. In 1943, the note was revised for new publications: "un patriote" was changed to "quelques gens de lettres patriotes," and "sous l'occupation nazie" became simply "sous l'oppression" (Thomas, *Contes*). Significantly, the word "Nazi" was never replaced with "allemand" because the contributors decided not to treat the terms as synonyms. The anti-Nazi German soldier Hans in Thomas's story "Le tilleul" embodies the distinction between the terms. As Thomas points out in the testimony collected in *La Résistance intellectuelle*, the literature of the Resistance was written to fight against an ideology of human degradation; it refused to characterize a racial or national difference, the French in opposition to the Germans ("Édith Thomas" 61). For Thomas, the defeat of German civilization in 1933, when Adolf Hitler came to power in Germany, was no less real than the military defeat of France in 1940.

Les Éditions de Minuit published thirty-three books between February 1942 and the liberation of Paris in August 1944; each one had the same elegant presentation and was small enough to fit into a coat pocket. Thomas took pleasure in registering the copyright of each volume at the Bibliothèque Nationale, where she worked, without the knowledge of either her comrades or the head administrator at the library, Bernard Faÿ, an enthusiastic Nazi collaborator who had been appointed to replace Julien Cain, who was Jewish.

For a long time Thomas had been determined to make contact with the Francs-Tireurs et Partisans, the Communist-led guerrilla group featured in "FTP," the final story in *Contes d'Auxois*, so that she could write about them for the clandestine press. Thomas's diary entry for 30 April 1944 consists only of a series of dashes to mark the date of her departure for the maquis, which she had been preparing to join for many months with the help of Resistance comrades. She made contact with the Francs-Tireurs et Partisans in the Cévennes Mountains of southern France and published the first account of her experience in *Les lettres françaises* in June 1944, a few weeks before the liberation of Paris.

Thomas's courage in the Resistance was prefigured in her personal struggle with extreme illness. In 1931, when Thomas was twenty-two years old, she was diagnosed with tuberculosis of the bone, a disease that attacked her knee, keeping her bedridden and in intense pain for three years. The ordeal left her in fragile health, with a permanent limp. From that period of distress, she developed a fierce and ongoing determination to give her life meaning. During the traumatic years of Nazi occupation, Thomas found that meaning in her choice to resist—to say no—with the force she had: the written word.

Note

1. See Kaufmann 87 for a reproduction of page 1 of the second issue of *Les lettres françaises*.

Works Cited

Bellanger, Claude. *La presse clandestine, 1940–1944*. Armand Colin, 1962.

Kaufmann, Dorothy. *Édith Thomas: A Passion for Resistance*. Cornell UP, 2004.

Thomas, Édith. *Contes d'Auxois*. Les Éditions de Minuit, 1943.

———. "Crier la verité!" *Les lettres françaises*, no. 2, Oct. 1942, pp. 1–2.

———. "Édith Thomas nous apporte quelques précisions." *La Résistance intellectuelle*, edited by Jacques Debû-Bridel, Juillard, 1970, pp. 54–64.

———. *Pages de journal, 1939–1944.* Pages de journal, 1939–1944, *suivies de* Journal intime de monsieur Célestin Costedet, edited by Dorothy Kaufmann, Éditions Viviane Hamy, 1995, pp. 37–221.

Vercors (Jean Bruller). *Le silence de la mer.* Les Éditions de Minuit, 1942.

Introduction

Michelle Chilcoat and Lori J. Marso

Édith Thomas: Restoring Women to the History of French Resistance

Working as archivist and then as senior conservator in the Archives Nationales in Paris for most of her adult life, Édith Thomas was an accomplished novelist, poet, short story writer, journalist, and pioneer in the discipline of women's history. Thomas must also be counted among a number of women whose participation in the French Resistance was without question crucial to the liberation of France. But to appreciate the significance of Thomas's contribution to the cause, one must consider the developing history of women in the Resistance.

Many factors have contributed to our increased understanding of how women participated in resisting Vichy-Nazi and then Nazi rule. Factors contributing to this greater understanding have included the ever-mounting urgency in locating and hearing firsthand from the last living witnesses to those events, the 2015 opening of World War II–era archives to the public, and the rapid digitization of materials in those archives and their accessibility through the Internet (as well as, for documents not yet digitized, indications on the Internet of where they are held and how they might be consulted). The year 2015 was also notable for the commemoration of two female members of the French Resistance,

Germaine Tillion and Charles de Gaulle's niece Geneviève de Gaulle-Anthonioz, whose remains were interred in the Panthéon for their crucial efforts in the liberation.

If the roles women played in the French Resistance have taken such a long time to become a sustained subject of historical and political attention, it is in part because of a longstanding belief, including among many French women, that even if they did participate actively, it would not be womanly to say so (unless their participation entailed nursing or knitting socks for the men in the Resistance). Silent and invisible behind the man or men in her life, a good French woman, according to this belief, was self-effacing, a martyr to the cause who might not even see herself as such. War was understood to involve men, not women; the *femme guerrière* was seen as no longer a woman and certainly not a man, but instead an aberration. Yet in the wake of two world wars, it was undeniable that women had had to fill the shoes of the men who went off to fight those wars and that women had demonstrated that they could indeed do anything men did when the situation demanded it.

And for a brief moment after the liberation of Paris, a few of the women who had played active parts throughout the Resistance were officially recognized for their contributions alongside their far more numerous fellow *combattants de l'ombre*, as Resistance fighters were commonly called. Newsreel footage shows, for example, twenty-year-old Madeleine Riffaud sitting atop a tank and waving to the jubilant crowds that lined Paris streets to welcome their liberators in 1944.[1] Between 1940 and 1945, six women were among the 1,036 people awarded the Croix de la Libération (World War II's most prestigious decoration).[2] Some *femmes résistantes* were even appointed delegates of the Assemblée Consultative Provisoire (Provisionary Consultative Assembly), including

Lucie Aubrac,[3] Gilberte Brossolette, Marie-Hélène Lefaucheux, Marthe Simard, and Marie-Claude Vaillant-Couturier.[4] Recognizing that many women had joined the secret work of the Resistance in the country's fight for freedom and had "payé un lourd tribut à la barbarie nazie," including as "combattantes des barricades," a Parisian campaign poster encouraged women, who would be exercising their newly won right to vote for the first time in the 1945 municipal elections, to run for office so as to "continuer votre participation dans la vie nationale" (qtd. in Musée 242). Several women ran in 1945 for seats in the first Assembly of the Fourth Republic, but women took only five percent of the seats, and unfortunately, they took a progressively smaller proportion in the ensuing years (Quétel 232).

Since then, the *femmes résistantes* have had a harder time retaining their place in the annals of French history. Of course, the history of the Resistance has always been difficult to recover because resistance activity is by its nature clandestine and because those who participated in the Resistance did so under pseudonyms or completely anonymously. But identifying the women who participated in the making of that history is further complicated by the ambiguities of gender. Disguising herself in an exaggerated femininity to distract Vichy officials, for example, a *femme résistante* could carry out resistance activities right under their noses. On the other hand, *femmes résistantes* often played down or masked their femininity when among male resistance fighters, who likely resented the presence of women in their ranks. While both tactics facilitated the active participation of *femmes résistantes* in the Resistance, both also contributed to their invisibility, making it easier for subsequent histories of the Resistance to ignore them.

Nevertheless, as a result of the increased focus on women in commemorations of the seventieth anniversary of the liberation of France and the seventy-fifth anniversary of the Normandy landings, the nature of resistance activity more broadly has been reassessed, and deified Resistance heroes such as Charles de Gaulle and Jean Moulin have been resituated within the context of the ordinary French people who made the liberation possible. These changes have been especially useful for reconsidering the two prevailing tendencies in understanding how the French people responded to their country's humiliating 1940 defeat by Nazi Germany. The first tendency, dominant from the beginning of the liberation in 1944 to the December 1964 transferal of Moulin's ashes to the Panthéon under de Gaulle's presidency, held that a majority of the French supported the Resistance and united behind it. The second tendency, emerging on the heels of the May 1968 mass student and worker demonstrations against the reigning hierarchies of social and political power, sought to expose the extent of French collaboration during the occupation years. In *Les résistants: L'histoire de ceux qui refusèrent*, Robert Belot suggests (5) that this latter tendency culminated in the decision by the Archives Nationales to commemorate the seventieth anniversary of the country's liberation with its exhibition *La collaboration (1940–1945)*, the first of its kind in France.

Les résistants is an important publication in that it represents an antidote to the tendencies described above: it endeavors to situate the Resistance "dans toute sa complexité, dans toute sa diversité," namely through a focus on the men and women "qui l'ont faite" but who were at the same time often motivated by "des rivalités, des divergences de conception, des ambitions humaines, trop humaines" (Belot 5). *Les résistants* also broadens and refines what it meant to resist in World War II France by approaching resistance activity in terms of three principle functions, "la propagande, le renseignement, et l'action paramilitaire." More significantly, perhaps, the study recounts how resistance propaganda produced at the beginning of the occupation laid the groundwork for the Resistance's intelligence and paramilitary action (37). With all media (print, radio, cinema, etc.) under their strict control and censorship, Vichy and occupation forces attempted to isolate France from the rest of the world, launching a massive propaganda campaign aimed at terrorizing the French into believing that the Vichy-Nazi collaboration represented their only hope against Communists and Jews—who, according to the fascists, were the real enemies.

The Resistance, therefore, first had to fight a psychological war aimed at shifting the mentality of a civilian population that, in the absence of reliable information, was either apathetic toward, or believed it had to resign itself to, the devastating defeat by the German army, which took 1.8 million French soldiers as prisoners of war. Yet even before Adolf Hitler declared war on the country, there were men and women in France who had been deeply concerned by the rise of fascist movements throughout Europe over the previous decade of economic crisis and who had, for example, fought in the Spanish Civil War or founded and written for newspapers in order to keep the public informed of the fascist threat. Thus, in Philippe Pétain's announcement of armistice and then of collaboration between Germany and France, these French people saw nothing less than the enslavement of their country under Nazi rule. Thomas must be included among these men and women whose voices and writings contributed early on to resistance against the rising wave of fascism across Europe.

Lost in the shadows of more famous intellectual power couples such as Simone de Beauvoir and Jean-Paul Sartre, and Elsa Triolet and Louis Aragon, Thomas remains largely unfamiliar to both French and English readers. To remedy this situation, Dorothy Kaufmann's impressively documented 2004 biography, *Édith Thomas: A Passion for Resistance* (translated into French in 2007), provides the historical, political, and literary contexts, as well as the particular life circumstances, that shaped Thomas's writings. Kaufmann's thorough archival research and numerous interviews with Thomas's colleagues, friends, and family members reveal Thomas in her many dimensions. For instance, Thomas did not fear solitude but actively set herself apart in situations that she believed called for an open demonstration of her commitment to a principled life. Born to nonpracticing Catholic parents who, while politically conservative, were open-minded and tolerant, she describes becoming a Protestant at age sixteen not as an expression of rebellion or religious belief but more succinctly as "le premier acte de ma liberté" (*Témoin compromis* 40) She would continue to enact this freedom, which she understood as exercising the capacity to think and act independently of others, even at the risk of incurring emotional or physical injury. In fact, commitment in and of itself was a guiding principle for Thomas throughout her life.

Fascism was on the rise across Europe when the twenty-year-old Thomas entered the École Nationale des Chartes in 1929 to pursue a degree in medieval history and archival studies. Her open hostility toward the extreme right singled her out in the conservative Catholic milieu. Diagnosed with tuberculosis of the bone after graduating in 1931 (and having contended with intense and persistent pain in her left knee throughout her studies), Thomas spent the greater part of the following two years in isolation and confined to bed. During that time, she discovered communism and her need to write, producing manuscripts for two novels, *La mort de Marie* and *L'homme criminal*. *La mort de Marie*, a haunting account of the main character's lonely yet ecstatic suffering and death by tuberculosis, received France's Prix de premier roman; both works were published in 1934 by Éditions Gallimard (still one of France's most prestigious presses).

Her long bout with a potentially fatal illness left Thomas emotionally and physically exhausted and permanently handicapped. Considering herself unmarriageable as an independent-minded and now disabled woman, Thomas questioned the point of her existence when she was so financially precarious that her main preoccupation involved insuring her next meal. Profound depression and suicidal thoughts, however, fueled Thomas's resolve to revolt against suffering, hers and that of others, especially after she witnessed the brutalities of French colonialism during a brief period she spent recuperating in Algeria in 1934. Upon her return to France, she sought work writing for left-wing newspapers in Paris; the newly founded anti-fascist newspaper *Vendredi* published her first articles, a series on the hardships particular to women workers. Brief membership in the Association des Écrivains et Artistes Révolutionnaires connected her with the surrealist author Louis Aragon, who hired her as a journalist for the Communist newspaper he published, *Ce Soir.* Between 1935 and 1938, Thomas contributed numerous articles on social problems in Paris, including the lamentable living conditions of aged workers and the need for health and education programs for impoverished children. Despite her limp and her fragile health, she also took on dangerous assignments, in Spain reporting for the Republican side of the Spanish Civil War, and in Austria carrying out secret interviews on the rise of Nazism in the year preceding the Anschluss.

Just after Aragon fired her from *Ce Soir* in mid-1938 because of differences of opinion related to his hardline communism, Thomas contracted tuberculosis again, of the lungs this time, and had to leave Paris for another long, painful treatment. In September 1941, Thomas returned to an occupied Paris, fully committed to fighting Hitler and Nazism. Despite misgivings stemming in part from her experiences with Aragon, she joined the Communist Party in 1942, as it offered the best way to hook up with the Resistance, which she had become determined to do the moment she learned of its activity. That same year, after the Gestapo arrested and executed Jacques Decour, the original editor of the clandestine newspaper *Les lettres françaises*, before he could get the first issue out, Thomas signed on as coeditor (anonymously of course). She composed hard-hitting yet compassionate articles for the paper such as "Crier la vérité!," in which she excoriates French literati who feel obliged as artists to "s'isoler dans [leur] tour d'ivoire," refusing to break their silence even as the cattle car of a French train passes them by, filled with children whose cries for "Maman" go unanswered. As Kaufmann mentions in her foreword to this volume, Thomas also contributed reports on the activity of Resistance fighters in several maquis groups throughout France after managing to visit them in spring 1944. The sole woman on the Comité National des Écrivains, which also included Sartre and Albert Camus, among others, Thomas opened her apartment at 15 rue Pierre Nicole (in the fifth arrondissement) to meetings of the intellectual resistance from February 1943 until the liberation. A commemorative plaque, installed in March 2013 at that address, now reminds passersby that Thomas risked her life to host such meetings, since hosting them was a crime punishable by execution under Nazi law, and in August 2019—seventy-five years after the liberation of Paris—the Place Édith Thomas was established at the Porte d'Orléans (fig. 1).[5]

Thomas also took part, along with Pierre de Lescure, Jean Bruller (better known by his pen name, Vercors), and Yvonne

Figure 1. Place Édith Thomas. Photograph by Michelle Chilcoat.

Paraf, in establishing Les Éditions de Minuit and helped distribute its publications at the risk of arrest, deportation, and execution.[6] In 1943, after the 1942 publication of Vercor's international bestseller *Le silence de la mer*, the press published Thomas's pseudonymous *Contes d'Auxois*, republished in this volume as *Stories of Resistance*, a collection of seven short stories that narrate extraordinary acts of resistance by ordinary people whom Thomas had personal knowledge of. Upon word of the liberation of France's capital in August 1944, Thomas dared to leave her Paris apartment, as bullets continued to fly, in order to take notes on the event directly from the barricades; 1945 saw the publication of her book *La libération de Paris*, which is based on her eyewitness account. She also completed a biography of Joan of Arc, which she undertook in order to redeem the woman warrior from the far right's exploitative depiction of her. At the Communist Party's behest Thomas also agreed to edit *Femmes françaises*, a journal for the Union des Femmes Françaises, from which she would resign immediately after the war because she was unable to cope with the editorial board's limiting of women's issues to concerns for family and household.

Between 1947 and 1949, Thomas experienced two great heartbreaks. The first was the ending of a brief but intense love affair with the Éditions Gallimard editor Dominique Aury (with whom Thomas nevertheless remained in close contact for the rest of her life). Aury was the woman who anonymously authored *Histoire d'O*, a highly controversial novel featuring female masochistic erotica and a character partly inspired by Thomas. The second heartbreak came with Thomas's decision—provoked by the Tito affair—to resign from the Communist Party.[7] Thomas harbored no illusions regarding the social death she would experience the moment she quit the party in 1949, and contrary to most of those who left the party, Thomas did so openly, in a letter published on 15 December in the leftist newspaper *Combat*.

Resisting the suicidal thoughts that arose within her once again, Thomas wrote several impressively documented historical biographies of powerful nineteenth-century women, including George Sand, Pauline Roland, and Louise Michel, distinguishing herself as a pioneer in the discipline of women's history. In almost all her writing, she turned to fictional characters or real people with whom she identified but who were uniquely shaped by their circumstances and particular moment in history. Thomas's own circumstances and moment aligned perhaps most closely with the main character of her last novel, published shortly before she died suddenly from viral hepatitis in 1970. In *Le jeu d'échecs*, despite the potentially pessimistic title (which translates literally as *The Game of Failures*), the main character, Aude, who is resolutely single and has just given birth to a little girl, finally sees that the reason for existence is "l'aventure d'amener au monde cette possibilité d'être humain" (265). This challenge was especially great for women, who struggled to find their place in a world created by and for men.

Thomas's unique approach to feminism runs through her publications—which, beyond seven novels, two short story collections, and six historical biographies, include hundreds of articles and reviews written for newspapers, journals, and magazines, academic as well as popular—although Thomas, much like her contemporary Simone de Beauvoir, considered the term *feminism* an outdated reference to the political and social demands of "nos grands-mères" (*Témoin compromis* 118). Thomas referred instead to "l'humanisme féminin," a concept that was already being formed in her first publication, *La mort de Marie*, and that crystallized in *Le jeu d'échecs* when Aude refers to "la solidarité des femmes entre elles, dans un univers qu'elles n'ont pas fait" (*Jeu* 261); earlier Aude observes that "[s]ans doute est-il plus facile d'être un homme qu'une femme, car il nous faut tout inventer" (255). But Aude, whose life trajectory mimics Thomas's very closely, is neither bitter nor despairing here. The competitive disadvantage that has been women's lot throughout history has only rendered the so-called weaker sex that much more remarkable. Furthermore, each generation of women is deeply indebted to the one that came before for the particular improvements it currently enjoys. It is in this vein that Aude remarks: "Il y a seulement cinquante ans, je n'aurais pu être celle que j'étais aujourd'hui : si consceinte, si volontaire, si responsable" (255–56).

But it is not just as an expression of gratitude that Thomas trained her historian's eye on the strong women whose actions ensured better conditions for her generation; Thomas also saw the historian's task as being to take account of what has already been done so that other people—women especially—can focus instead on realizing the "possibilité d'être humain" (*Jeu* 265). But the condition of being human cannot be achieved as long as there is war, which reduces people to the status of nonhuman animals who must struggle to meet their most basic needs, an idea clearly expressed in the first of Thomas's seven stories in *Contes d'Auxois*.

Everyday Acts of Resistance: Thomas's *Contes d'Auxois*

Contes d'Auxois introduces readers to a host of ordinary characters living through the extraordinary times of France under Nazi occupation. Each story, "transcrit du réel," as indicated on the title page of the 1943 Les Éditions de Minuit edition, explores the varying ways in which the characters respond to the pathological exigencies of Vichy collaborationist rule and to relentless Nazi propaganda. Confronted with their own suffering—as well as the knowledge that declared enemies of the state, including children, were being arrested, held under horrific conditions, tortured, and murdered—these characters act, in their everyday lives, in ways that challenge notions of what is heroic and what is simply human. In these stories, Thomas writes of the ordinary people, things, and situations that history tends to overlook. Readers are likely to see themselves in the lives and daily dilemmas of these characters, who, despite being unremarkable in many respects, recognize the possibility of human solidarity precisely because of the drastically reduced opportunities they have for expressing that solidarity.

Among the major preoccupations of many French intellectuals during and after the war years were the ethical and political quandaries that arose from living under the occupation. Not surprisingly, many of these intellectuals focused on determining which kinds of actions and behaviors constituted resistance to or cooperation with Nazi authorities, and what their ethical justifications could be. For example, Beauvoir, a contemporary of Thomas, wrote her famous wartime novel *Le sang des autres* to address explicitly whether violence can be ethically justified when employed in the name of furthering freedom. Interestingly, Thomas and Beauvoir never met, even though Beauvoir was Sartre's partner and Thomas was a comrade of Sartre's on the Comité National des Écrivains; while both women were prolific writers on the French political left who lived through and wrote about World War II, the occupation, the trials of collaborators, debates over the meaning of Joseph Stalin's crimes, and the Algerian War, only Beauvoir achieved great literary fame, both in her time and to this day.

To appreciate the political, literary, historical, and ethical weight of Thomas's wartime writings, particularly her short stories in *Contes d'Auxois*, one may draw a comparison to Beauvoir's account of the occupation and the Resistance in *Le sang des autres*. One of the central themes in this novel is that individuals are never absolutely free, since they exist in a web of relationships in which every human choice has an impact, often unpredictable, on others both known and unknown. Beauvoir's fictional account of the occupation illustrates what happens when people engage in bad faith despite or even because of this central fact of existence. Hélène, one of the novel's main characters, lies in bed dying from an injury sustained when she attempted to carry out a violent attack on occupying German soldiers. By her bedside is Jean, a Resistance leader who reflects in anguish on his role in Hélène's impending death. His reflections are complicated by his sense of responsibility for both her individual happiness and the greater cause of French freedom. The novel is constructed mainly as a series of flashbacks, which consist of dialogues between various characters and interior monologues that ponder the potentially adverse effects of human choices.

By comparison, Thomas's stories bear witness to characters who respond to a wide variety of situations, from a woman who mutters her disgust as a German soldier passes by while she waits in the bitter cold for food supplies that will most likely run out before she gets through the line; to two young men who, despite the horrid conditions of the German work camp they have escaped, keep their promise to tell the French that not all Germans side with the Nazis and who also wonder if life after their adventure can still hold meaning for them; to a middle-aged woman who makes a cup of tea for an occupying soldier who has come down with a cold, because at that moment she sees him as some mother's son rather than as an enemy; and to six men who come together for very different reasons, risking their lives as they carry out an act of sabotage against German soldiers.

Beauvoir's use of a limited set of highly dramatic characters in extreme situations thus stands in stark contrast to Thomas's focus on ordinary people and everyday acts of resistance. For Beauvoir, fiction provides the opportunity for creating the exemplary situation necessary to illustrate the most important ethical question of life under the occupation, which is the choice to act or not act when one is aware that every choice means another human will be affected, very likely in negative ways. Beauvoir's exclusive focus on great acts of resistance that are defined above all by political subversion and violence obscures many other ethical issues that arise in the day-to-day lives of ordinary citizens, issues that are deftly portrayed by Thomas. Offering a slice of life from this time period in France, Thomas's stories in *Contes d'Auxois* play out the real choices made by people to counter the more mundane forms of brute authority that appeared under the occupation, and the stories underscore the inevitability of human responsibility toward both intimates and strangers.

Still another important difference between Thomas's and Beauvoir's World War II writing has to do with each author's level of personal engagement. Quite simply, Beauvoir did not engage in the efforts of the Resistance, whereas Thomas did. While Beauvoir sat at her table in a Paris café writing *Le sang des autres*, which she did not publish until after the war, Thomas actively wrote, published, and hosted meetings throughout the war. Thus Thomas's writing communicates a more immediate sense of how ordinary people make choices under oppressive rule. Whereas Beauvoir's ethics is most aptly understood as philosophical and abstract, Thomas's is better described as situational and concrete.

Unlike the writings of Beauvoir or Sartre from that time, in which formal existential questions play a central role, Thomas's seven stories are less distinctly linked to one particular school of philosophical thought. They instead constitute everyday ethics, an ethics that applies not only when times are extraordinary but also when they are not. These stories inspire readers to ask themselves questions like the following: How can small acts of resistance against the illegitimate imposition of authority increase feelings of solidarity among human beings? What might those identified as enemy occupiers share in the struggle against human degradation? And where and how do individuals find solidarity in a world in which the growing potential for human connectivity can also isolate and overwhelm? This two-volume edition of *Contes d'Auxois*, which presents the original French and the first English translation of the work in its entirety, will provide readers of both languages a rich opportunity to discover Thomas's important and original representations of the more ordinary truths of resistance and collaboration, as well as of the vast gray area between them.

Notes

1. This footage appears in the 2015 documentary *Résistantes,* in which Madeleine Riffaud, Cécile Rol-Tanguy, and Marie-José Chombart de Lauwe recount their experiences in the Resistance. In their nineties when they were interviewed, all three were about twenty when they joined the Resistance. Riffaud, a member of the Francs-Tireurs et Partisans, is among the few acknowledged French *femmes résistantes* who took up arms. She was captured, tortured, and sentenced to death by the Gestapo for gunning down a German soldier in Paris, by the Seine, in broad daylight. Miraculously, she was freed from prison in time to join friends fighting to liberate Paris; they took eighty German prisoners.

2. The militant feminist and anti-fascist Berty Albrecht was one of the six women awarded this honor. Albrecht and her partner Henri Frenay founded the Combat resistance network for moving Resistance fighters and escaped prisoners across the demarcation line between occupied France and the free zone. They also founded several underground newspapers, including the well-known *Combat.* Arrested and tortured by the Gestapo in 1943, Albrecht chose to hang herself rather than risk naming any members of the network. In 1947 Thomas published her *Berthie Albrecht, Pierre Arrighi, Général Brosset, D. Corticchiato, Jean Prévost: Cinq parmi d'autres,* a preview of her pioneering work in forging the field of women's history.

3. In 1940, Lucie Aubrac and her husband Raymond Aubrac formed a small Resistance group that carried out railway sabotage, distributed tracts about the Resistance, and helped fellow *résistants* escape arrest. Aubrac is perhaps best known for successfully orchestrating her husband's escape from prison.

4. Soon after the French government banned Communism and its presses in 1939, Vaillant-Couturier participated in resistance activity, overseeing the clandestine production of Communist Party publications including *L'humanité.* She also coordinated communications among intellectual and armed Resistance groups. Arrested in February 1942, she was deported to Auschwitz-Birkenau in January 1943, in a group of two hundred and thirty *femmes résistantes* that included Danielle Casanova. Casanova joined the Communist Youth League while

studying to become a dental surgeon. An ardent anti-fascist activist, Casanova contributed to clandestine presses, founded clandestine women's resistance journals, and organized demonstrations against Vichy and Nazi rule. Arrested in 1942, Casanova continued her political organizing while in Auschwitz until her death from typhus in May 1943. Thomas honored these women in her poem "Pour celles du camp d'Auschwitz," anonymously published in the December 1943 issue of *Les lettres françaises.*

5. The plaque and the honorific street name are the results of the efforts of Thomas's nephew Daniel Thomas.

6. For more on Thomas's work for Les Éditions de Minuit, see Kaufmann's foreword in this volume.

7. When the Yugoslav dictator Josip Tito broke ties with the Soviet Union, the French Communist Party began a six-year campaign against Tito and Yugoslavia for resisting subjugation by Stalin.

Works Cited

Beauvoir, Simone de. *Le sang des autres.* Éditions Gallimard, 1945.

Belot, Robert. *Les résistants: L'histoire de ceux qui refusèrent.* Larousse, 2015.

Kaufmann, Dorothy. *Édith Thomas: A Passion for Resistance.* Cornell UP, 2004.

Musée de la Résistance Nationale. *Les résistants, 1940–1945: Récits, témoignages et documents inédits du Musée de la Résistance Nationale.* Éditions Belin, 2015.

Quétel, Claude. *Femmes dans la guerre, 1939–1945.* Larousse, 2007.

Résistantes. Directed by Pierre Hurel, featuring Madeleine Riffaud et al., Arte, 2015.

Thomas, Édith. *Contes d'Auxois.* Les Éditions de Minuit, 1943.

———. "Crier la vérité!" *Les lettres françaises,* no. 2, Oct. 1942, pp. 1–2.

———. "L'humanisme féminin." 1949. Papiers Édith Thomas, 318AP3, Archives Nationales, Paris.

———. *Le jeu d'échecs.* Grasset, 1970.

———. "Pour celles du camp d'Auschwitz." *Les lettres françaises,* no. 12, Dec. 1943, p. 3.

———. *Le témoin compromis.* Éditions Viviane Hamy, 1995.

Bibliography of Works by Édith Thomas

Novels

Le champ libre. Éditions Gallimard, 1945.

Étude de femmes. Éditions Colbert, 1945.

L'homme criminel. Éditions Gallimard, 1934.

Le jeu d'échecs. 1970. 2nd ed., Éditions Viviane Hamy, 2018.

La mort de Marie. Éditions Gallimard, 1934.

Le refus. Éditions Sociales Internationales, 1936.

Sept–sorts. Éditions Gallimard, 1935.

Short Story Collections

Contes d'Auxois. Les Éditions de Minuit, 1943.

Ève et les autres. 1952. Mercure de France, 1970.

Essay Collections, Biographies, and Historical Studies

Berthie Albrecht, Pierre Arrighi, Général Brosset, D. Corticchiato, Jean Prévost: Cinq parmi d'autres. Les Éditions de Minuit, 1947.

Les femmes de 1848. PU de France, 1948.

George Sand. Éditions Universitaires, 1960.

Jeanne d'Arc. 1947. 2nd ed., Éditions Gallimard, 1952.

La libération de Paris. Photographs by Robert Doisneau, et al., Éditions Mellottée, 1945.

Louise Michel ou la Velléda de l'anarchie. Éditions Gallimard, 1971.

Pauline Roland: Socialisme et féminisme au XIXe siècle. Librarie Marcel Rivière, 1956.

Les "pétroleuses." Éditions Gallimard, 1963.

Rossel, 1844–1871. Éditions Gallimard, 1967.

Other Works

Pages de journal, 1939–1944, *suivies de* Journal intime de monsieur Célestin Costedet. Edited by Dorothy Kaufmann, Éditions Viviane Hamy, 1995.

Le témoin compromis. 1952. Edited by Dorothy Kaufmann, Éditions Viviane Hamy, 1995.

English Translations

Eve and the Others. Translated by Estelle Eirinberg, Continental Editions, 1976.

"F.T.P." Translated by Alistair Hamilton. *Defeat and Beyond: An Anthology of French Wartime Writing, 1940–1945*, edited by Germaine Brée and George Bernauer, Pantheon Books, 1970.

Louise Michel. Translated by Penelope Williams, Black Rose Books, 1980.

"The Professor and the Mussels." Translated by Maria Jolas. *Bedside Book of Famous French Stories*, edited by Belle Becker and Robert Linscott, Random House, 1945.

The Women Incendiaries. Translated by James Atkinson and Starr Atkinson, paperback ed., Haymarket Books, 2007.

Selected Criticism and Commentary on Édith Thomas

Baty-Delande, Hélène. "Militantes: Quelles représentations de l'engagement au féminin? Sur *La femme vierge* de Madeleine Pelletier, *Délivrance* de Louise Weiss et *Le refus* d'Édith Thomas." *Journalisme et littérature de la gauche des années 1930*, edited by Anne Mathieu and François Ouellet, PU de Rennes, 2014, pp. 191–202.

Chilcoat, Michelle. "Édith Thomas (1909–1970)." *Fifty-One Key Feminist Thinkers*, edited by Lori J. Marso, Routledge, 2016, pp. 222–27.

Kaufmann, Dorothy. *Édith Thomas: A Passion for Resistance.* Cornell UP, 2004.

———. *Édith Thomas: Passionnément résistante.* Translated by Danielle Wargny, Éditions Autrement, 2007.

———. "L'humanisme féminin." *Intellectuelles: Du genre en histoire des intellectuels*, edited by Nicole Racine and Michel Trebitsch, Éditions Complexe, 2004, pp. 177–89.

———. "The Story of Two Women: Dominique Aury and Édith Thomas." *Signs*, vol. 23, no. 4, Summer 1998, pp. 883–905.

———. "Uncovering a Woman's Life: Édith Thomas (Novelist, Historian, *Résistante*)." *The French Review*, vol. 67, no. 1, Oct. 1993, pp. 61–72.

Kershaw, Angela. "Autodidacticism and Criminality in Jean-Paul Sartre's *La nausée* and Édith Thomas's *L'homme criminel*." *The Modern Language Review*, vol. 96, no. 3, July 2001, pp. 679–92.

O'Flaherty, Angela. "La Résistance Féminine: An Analysis of the Representation of Women in Selected Wartime Texts by Édith Thomas and Elsa Triolet." *French and Francophone Women Facing War / Les femmes face à la guerre*, edited by Alison S. Fell, Peter Lang, 2009, pp. 41–57.

Rochester, Myrna Bell, and Mary Lawrence Test. "Words as Hammers, Words as Bullets: Committed Fiction and French Women Writers of the Occupation Years." *Dalhousie French Studies*, vol. 54, Spring 2001, pp. 90–102.

Note on the Text

The French text in this volume is taken from the 1945 edition of Édith Thomas's *Contes d'Auxois*, which is identical to the edition originally published under repressive conditions in Paris on 10 December 1943. The footnotes that accompany the text are in large part the result of discussions with Daniel Thomas, Édith Thomas's nephew and coexecutor of Thomas's literary estate, and Dorothy Kaufmann, Édith Thomas's biographer.

Contes d'Auxois

Les moules et le professeur

Mon ami, dit Mme Poncelet en ouvrant la porte du bureau, mon ami, excuse-moi de te déranger.

Le vieux professeur leva la tête et posa sa plume sur un rond de feutre. Au delà de *l'Énéide*, il apercevait, dans une brume, le visage de sa femme. Puis, la brume disparut. Le vieillard fit un saut démesuré dans le temps et vit sa femme enveloppée d'un peignoir de pilou et d'un vieux manteau de drap noir remonté jusqu'aux oreilles, et vit le doux visage flétri de sa femme qui réfléchissait comme un miroir le sourire secret qu'elle avait déjà à vingt-cinq ans, quand il l'avait épousée, parce que ce sourire secret était devenu peu à peu indispensable à sa vie, et l'était resté depuis.

— Qu'y a-t-il, mon amie ? demanda-t-il.

— Il faudra que tu ailles voir si notre numéro de triperie est sorti, dit-elle.[1] Et peut-être, en revenant, pourras-tu t'arrêter à la poissonnerie.

---

1. Madame Poncelet's comment refers to the Vichy-imposed rationing system of 1940 that issued *cartes de ravitaillement* authorizing the holder to purchase indicated items (food, coal, gas, clothing, etc.) at specified times and in quantities that depended mainly on the individual's age, gender, and

— Je ferais mieux de m'arrêter d'abord à la poissonnerie, dit M. Poncelet.

— Comme tu voudras, mon ami.

Et elle retourna à la cuisine.

Il enfila sa pelisse de fourrure au col tout usé et enfonça un béret sur sa tête. On n'avait pas besoin de le tenir, même si le vent soufflait. C'était plus commode pour faire les queues. Et, après avoir jeté un regard mêlé de mélancolie, de regret et d'ironie peut-être, sur sa table de travail, il alla à la cuisine décrocher un sac de moleskine dont la poignée était raccommodée avec une ficelle.

— Tu ne vas pas laver la cuisine par ce froid, dit-il.

— On ne peut pourtant pas vivre dans la saleté tout l'hiver. Il y a un peu de détente, aujourd'hui.

Du feu, on en faisait seulement dans son bureau, parce qu'il fallait qu'il essayât de continuer son grand travail sur *Les origines de* l'Enéide — le grand travail de toute sa vie — parce qu'il fallait continuer. Malgré tout. Mais ils avaient transporté un divan dans le bureau et ils y dormaient, travaillaient, mangeaient et, sur un réchaud, faisaient la cuisine. Elle disait, en remuant une casserole :

— Je fais du bruit, pardonne-moi, mon ami.

Et il répondait :

---

profession. The system drastically reduced the daily food intake of much of the French population, from at best 1,700 calories at the beginning of the occupation to 1,200 or less by the end.

— Tu sais bien que tu ne me déranges jamais, mon amie. Nous sommes encore plus près l'un de l'autre à vivre sans cesse ainsi.

Non, ce n'était pas la fin de vie qu'il avait rêvée pour elle, ni pour lui. Non, ce n'était pas la fin de vie.

Bien qu'elle fût vieille et qu'elle eût parfois des crises cardiaques qui l'épouvantaient, il ne pouvait pas lui donner de domestique, ni même de femme de ménage : les Allemands les payaient beaucoup plus cher qu'un professeur en retraite ne le pouvait faire. Il ne pouvait pas davantage l'emmener passer les mois les plus noirs à Cannes ou à Nice, comme il le lui avait promis pour « le temps où il serait à la retraite » : il fallait franchir la ligne de démarcation qui coupait la France en deux ;[2] et la vie, de l'autre côté, était encore plus coûteuse qu'à Paris, à cause de tous ces gens riches qui s'y étaient installés pour la durée de la guerre. Et puis, à Paris, on se sentait résister. On résistait. Et le vieil homme, en se rendant à la poissonnerie, contre le vent qui lui sciait en deux le visage — où donc Annette avait-elle aperçu une détente ? — n'était pas loin de penser que, lui aussi, il accomplissait un acte de

---

2. Established by the armistice of June 1940 after France fell to the Germans, a 1,200-kilometer *ligne de démarcation* divided Nazi-occupied France in the north and west from the so-called free zone in the southeast, which the Vichy government administered under the leadership of the *maréchal* Philippe Pétain. By March 1943, all of France was under Nazi occupation.

résistance, était un maillon infime, mais nécessaire, dans l'enchaînement rigoureux de l'histoire.

Déjà, une longue file patientait sur le trottoir, une longue file faite de femmes emmitouflées, avec des foulards de tête noués sous le menton. Elles étaient collées à la grille encore fermée de la poissonnerie, comme des fourmis sur un cadavre de ver de terre. Et que sommes-nous de plus que des fourmis qui vont, cherchant leur nourriture, des fourmis dont la fourmilière a été bouleversée d'un coup de botte ? Ce n'était pas une comparaison bien originale. M. Poncelet s'en apercevait. Mais allez donc en trouver une autre, par ce froid et ce vent ? D'ailleurs, ramenés sans cesse à ces préoccupations de feu et de nourriture, qu'étions-nous devenus de plus que des animaux ? L'homme commence après. Il songea un instant à son grand ouvrage sur *Les origines de* l'Enéide qui était pour lui la fin et la justification de sa vie, et haussa les épaules.

Autour de lui, il voyait des visages bleutés de froid. Il en connaissait certains, à force de les rencontrer tous les jours, attendant anxieusement à la porte des magasins. Il savait que le mari de cette jeune femme était prisonnier, qu'elle attendait son retour. Mais les jours, les mois, les années passaient dans l'attente, l'anxiété et la boue.[3] Il savait

3. Over 2.5 million French people spent time in German captivity during the war, either as forced laborers or prisoners of war. Most of the latter (around 1.5 million in total), who were taken in 1940, were not returned to France until 1945.

que cette vieille paysanne, avec ses lèvres serrées comme une bourse, était venue du fond des Pyrénées « faire les queues » pour sa fille qui travaillait en usine : « Quand on a deux enfants à nourrir, Monsieur, et un mari qui ne gagne même pas pour lui . . . »

Des nouvelles extravagantes circulaient, reprises sans cesse de bouche à oreille, et amplifiées. Le professeur voyait ainsi, à l'état naissant, la geste de tout un peuple s'organiser et se répandre.[4] Ce phénomène de tradition orale lui rappelait Homère ou la *Chanson de Roland,* et il souriait malgré le froid.

La grille de la poissonnerie était maintenant ouverte et il avançait d'un pas toutes les cinq minutes : c'était curieux de vivre.

De temps en temps, on entendait un bruit de bottes sur le trottoir. Un soldat en uniforme feld-grau passait. Derrière lui, une femme disait :

---

4. *La geste* is an ensemble of medieval epic poems that were recited before both elite and popular (i.e., illiterate) audiences and that recount, among other things, acts of wartime heroism meant to solidify a people's sense of themselves as a community or nation. *The Song of Roland* dates back to the eleventh or twelfth century and recounts a battle of Charlemagne's from the eighth century. *La geste* harks further back to classical epic poetry, such as that of Homer, as both are believed to have their origins in the oral tradition and may be either the works of individual authors or the collective and anonymous productions of a people. While these works have footing in history, how they are told and embellished is what determines their popularity and continued transmission.

— Les salauds, ce qu'il peut y en avoir, quand même. C'est comme les poux. Quand est-ce qu'on ne les verra plus ?

Et les autres approuvaient.

C'était le temps où, dans les journaux allemands écrits en français, on parlait de la collaboration entre la France et l'Allemagne. Mais le peuple ne s'y était pas laissé tromper. Il avait compris tout de suite — beaucoup plus vite et plus sûrement que les bourgeois, reconnaissait M. Poncelet — que cette collaboration était le nom d'une imposture et recouvrait la réduction en esclavage de tout un continent, la plus absolue sujétion que l'on eût vue depuis des siècles. On ne pourra songer à la collaboration véritable qu'après, lorsqu'on aura retrouvé l'homme, se disait M. Poncelet, en entendant s'éloigner le bruit des bottes. Et ce ne sont pas les maîtres qui l'établiront, cette collaboration, mais les peuples eux-mêmes, quand ils en auront assez de souffrir.

Voilà qu'il se croyait encore devant ses élèves, enfourchant pour eux le grand percheron tranquille de l'histoire.[5] Il sourit, se moquant de lui-même ; fit un pas.

---

5. A Percheron is a French breed of horse highly valued for its power, endurance, intelligence, and even temperament. Both heavy and quick, it is ideal for driving and hauling as well as for riding. From the Middle Ages through World War II, the Percheron featured in war, agriculture, transportation, and construction, after which it was replaced by technologies of the modernization it played an elemental role in bringing about.

Maintenant, on apercevait l'intérieur du magasin. On y voyait quelques grands paniers pleins de moules.

— Il y en aura bien pour tout le monde, dit une femme à côté de lui.

— Si les « priorités » n'arrivent pas, fit aigrement la vieille paysanne, desserrant un instant ses lèvres cousues. Si les « priorités » n'arrivent pas.[6] Comment voulez-vous qu'une mère ait jamais trois enfants, si on laisse mourir de faim les deux autres avant la venue du troisième ?[7]

Ce qui étonnait toujours le professeur, c'était le bon sens de ces femmes, et leur courage. Peu de plaintes. Une sorte de stoïcisme qui ne se connaissait point. Au fond, les êtres humains valaient beaucoup mieux qu'il ne le croyait, quand il restait chez lui, le nez dans ses livres. Qu'est-ce que tous ces êtres auraient donné en d'autres circonstances plus favorables à leur développement ? On n'en savait rien. Encore rien.

---

6. Those who stood in line had to deal not only with the interminable waits and the increasing likelihood that they would go home empty-handed, while a black market catered to the French elite, Vichy operatives, and German occupiers, but also with the fact that priority cards allowed pregnant and nursing women to be served first and to buy in greater quantities, which generated animosity among the shoppers, who were mainly women. While rioting did sometimes break out, as time wore on the lines increasingly provided opportunities for demonstrations—organized largely by women—against the Vichy and Nazi regimes.

7. The peasant woman's remark alludes to Pétain's relentless probirth campaign promising material rewards to families with three or more children.

Il avança d'un pas. Les paniers de moules se vidaient.

—— Il n'y en aura pas pour tout le monde, constata sa voisine.

Quelle aventure prodigieuse que l'homme ! songeait-il, bien que le vent s'engouffrât le long de la rue et vint lui couper le nez et les oreilles, bien qu'il fût saugrenu d'attendre des heures pour une livre de moules que, jadis, il n'aimait pas, et que *Les origines de* l'Enéide n'avançassent pas d'une ligne pendant ce temps-là.

—— Ce n'est plus la peine d'attendre, dit la femme à côté de lui : il n'y en aura pas pour nous.

Et, en effet, le dernier panier était déjà presque vide. Toutefois, M. Poncelet resta encore un peu, par scrupule intellectuel, par besoin de preuves et de vérifications. Quand la dernière moule eut disparu dans un cabas, le professeur s'en alla.

Il lui fallait encore passer à la triperie. Ce ne fut pas long ; son numéro n'était pas sorti. Le ravitaillement était une sorte de loterie où personne ne gagnait jamais. Alors, il retourna à petits pas vers sa maison, son vieux sac vide au bras.

— Eh bien, as-tu rapporté quelque chose, mon ami ?

— Non, répondit-il, confus malgré tout.

Il aurait dû partir un peu plus tôt, quitter de lui-même *l'Enéide,* ne pas attendre que sa femme l'en priât.

—— Mais tu es tout gelé, dit-elle, en lui prenant la main. Je vais te faire une infusion pour te réchauffer.

Il s'était remis à sa table de travail. Il entendait sa femme tourner autour du réchaud. Il sentait sa présence.

—— Prends un morceau de sucre, dit-elle.

Il savait qu'elle s'en privait pour lui. Il regarda son sourire secret, dont il connaissait la tendresse.

Oui, la vie était une aventure merveilleuse.

La relève

Dans les journaux, on lisait : «Ouvriers, partez pour l'Allemagne. C'est un devoir pour vous, qui n'avez pas connu la captivité des camps, d'aller relever ceux qui attendent anxieusement, depuis des mois, derrière des fils barbelés, le moment de leur délivrance. Etc . . . ».[1]

---

1. *La relève* is the euphemism used by the Vichy media campaign in early 1942 to pressure French workers to volunteer to go to Germany to replace German workers who had been mobilized and sent to the Russian front. Posters and front-page headlines publicized that for every three French workers (men or women) who went to work in Germany, one French prisoner of war would be returned to France. By September 1942, when it was clear the campaign had failed, the Vichy government legislated the *relève forcée*, which designated male workers aged eighteen to fifty and female workers aged twenty-one to thirty-five as "volunteers." In February 1943, the Vichy government enforced the infamous *service du travail obligatoire* (STO), applicable to all men born between 1 January 1920 and 31 December 1922. (Thomas's story, which doesn't mention the STO, was probably written before the policy was implemented.) Huge numbers of young French men headed for the maquis as a way of evading the STO. The French word *maquis* became synonymous with the Resistance because Resistance fighters—often called *maquisards*—hid in places that were difficult to access (i.e., mountainous or heavily wooded), where they strategized their attacks on the Nazis and on Nazi sympathizers and planned, above all, for the liberation of France.

La radio interdite scandait d'une voix mystérieuse autant qu'impérative qui s'incrustait dans les têtes : « En Allemagne, ne va pas, en Allemagne, ne va pas ».

Eux, discutaient dans les bistrots, au sortir des usines, dans les bistrots dont on savait que le patron n'était pas de la police et où l'on pouvait discuter sans crainte. Ils se sentaient libres. Encore libres de choisir : d'accepter ou de refuser. Libres de peser leur acte à la seule balance de leur conscience. Des hommes libres comme lorsqu'ils décidaient jadis de se mettre en grève et qu'ils opposaient leur force à l'autre force qui les opprimait, et qui apprenait peu à peu à les connaître en tant que force.

Depuis l'armistice,[2] c'était la première fois qu'ils avaient le choix d'agir, même si ce choix n'impliquait qu'une action négative, un refus.

— Moi, disait l'un, si je pouvais aller remplacer mon cousin qui est quasi mon frère, si je pouvais dire : je veux bien partir à la condition que vous libériez Merlin (Marcel), mon cousin qui est comme mon frère, alors, je partirais.

— Tu parles, répondait-on.

Un autre disait :

2. The armistice of June 1940. Hitler insisted on signing it in the same railway car that the November 1918 armistice of World War I had been signed in.

—— Mais tout de même, si on pouvait faire libérer quelqu'un, ça vaudrait la peine, même si on ne peut pas faire libérer ceux qu'on connaît.

Celui-là, on le tenait pour un bon garçon. On était sûr que ce n'était ni une mouche, ni un jaune, mais il n'avait aucun allant. Pendant les grèves de 36, il se contentait de dire : « Si vous êtes de cet avis ». Puis il marchait avec les autres. Son frère était jardinier chez la marquise de Loctudy, comme son père l'était, comme on l'était dans sa famille, de père en fils. Il pensait qu'il faut faire la volonté de Dieu et que la volonté des hommes n'est pas toujours la volonté de Dieu et la preuve, c'est que Dieu a voulu des pauvres et des riches, des gens qui travaillent et des gens pour qui l'on travaille : éternellement. El que les gens riches et puissants détiennent leur pouvoir de Dieu, puisqu'ils sont riches et puissants et qu'ils ne le seraient pas sans Sa volonté ; et que lui, Le Guirrec, dont la femme se mourait de tuberculose à l'Hôpital Laennec et dont les enfants étaient tous morts en bas âge, n'avait qu'à obéir aux riches et aux puissants, puisque Dieu, de toute évidence, avait voulu sa misère et son humilité ; maintenant il n'avait qu'à obéir au Maréchal.[3]

---

3. Referring to Pétain. In France, *maréchal* is a military honor, rather than a military rank. Pétain was granted the distinction for his military performance in World War I. Tried and sentenced to death for treason after World War II, he was stripped of all military ranks and honors, except for that of

— Mais tu obéis aux ordres des Allemands, lui objectait-on, car on savait qu'il était français et breton au moins autant que catholique.

— Je crois qu'il faut obéir au Maréchal, répondait-il avec obstination. Le Maréchal sait ce qu'il fait.

Pourtant Le Guirrec ne partait pas : il ne pouvait pas laisser sa femme mourir toute seule à l'hôpital. Il ne pouvait pas laisser son pays. Était-ce sa petite chambre en désordre — trop petite pour être en ordre — qui donnait sur les cheminées d'usine, les toits de tôle et les rails qui s'en allaient pour lui ? Ou bien, là-bas, la métairie que ses parents habitaient depuis des siècles et qui, malgré leur travail pendant des siècles, ne leur appartenait toujours pas ? Ou bien sa langue ? Mais ici non plus on ne parlait pas sa langue.[4] Bref, son pays.

Et Le Guirrec ne partait pas.

Il y en avait deux qui s'étaient engagés pour l'Allemagne, deux très jeunes et des cerveaux brûlés. Ce n'était pas par conviction qu'ils partaient, « pour sauver l'Europe du

maréchal. Because of Pétain's age (ninety at the time of his trial), President Charles de Gaulle commuted Pétain's sentence to life in prison.

4. The Jules Ferry laws of 1881 and 1882, lauded for making elementary education in France compulsory, free, and nonreligious, also banned all languages but French from the classroom, at a time when millions of children in France spoke only the language of their region. For decades after, children were humiliated and punished for speaking the only language they knew (e.g., Breton or Basque) when at school.

bolchevisme ». Ils s'en fichaient bien, du bolchevisme. Mais, parce que c'était la forme de l'aventure et du resquillage qui s'offrait actuellement à eux. C'étaient des resquilleurs, des gens en qui l'on ne pouvait pas avoir confiance. Et d'ailleurs de médiocres ouvriers, des bricoleurs plutôt. On en était content. Ce n'était pas des gars comme eux qui aideraient beaucoup à la victoire de l'Allemagne.

Dans les journaux, cependant, on constatait avec satisfaction le grand succès de la relève et que des trains partaient chaque jour pour l'Allemagne. Mais ici, on savait bien que deux ouvriers seulement s'étaient spontanément engagés. Et qu'à la conférence organisée par la Direction il n'en était venu que vingt-cinq sur plus de mille. Encore n'était-ce qu'après entente avec les autres et pour leur faire une relation exacte de ce qu'on y aurait raconté. Et si c'était ainsi chez nous, il n'y avait aucune raison de croire qu'il en allait ailleurs autrement, que chez Renault, ou chez Gnome et Rhône,[5] les copains montraient un plus grand empressement.

En effet, on s'aperçut bientôt que les appels se faisaient plus pressants, puis que les « volontaires » étaient désignés d'office, que l'on était volontaire obligatoire (de même qu'on appelait l'Allemagne, Europe ; la dictature des trusts, socialisme ; l'organisation de la disette, ravitaille-

5. Gnome et Rhône was a major aircraft engine manufacturer in France.

ment : il n'était pas nécessaire d'être académicien pour constater que les mots avaient changé de sens et qu'il fallait les prendre au rebours de ce qu'on croyait qu'ils signifiaient).

— Et toi, qu'est-ce que tu feras, si l'on te désigne ? se demandait-on entre soi pour la centième fois.

— Je ne partirai pas.

— C'est facile à dire. Mais où iras-tu ?

Et c'était bien là la question. Aller retrouver de Gaulle ?[6] Il y en avait qui racontaient que des chalutiers sortaient des ports avec un certain nombre d'hommes et revenaient avec le même nombre : mais ce n'étaient pas les mêmes visages. L'échange se faisait au large avec des bateaux anglais. Partir pour la zone libre et s'engager dans l'armée de l'armistice ? Cette armée de l'armistice ne leur disait rien qui vaille, avec tous ces généraux dont on n'avait jamais tant parlé que depuis qu'ils avaient été vaincus, cette armée de l'armistice qui était l'armée de la bourgeoisie triomphante et vaincue. D'ailleurs l'armée fut dissoute, la

---

6. Virtually unheard of in France when he was stationed in London and recognized by Britain as leader of the Forces Françaises Libres in 1940, General Charles de Gaulle first became familiar to the French as a voice on the BBC's Radio Londres exhorting the French to resist Nazi occupation. Besides boosting French morale and countering the onslaught of Nazi propaganda on Radio Paris and Radio Vichy, Radio Londres transmitted hundreds of coded messages that aided de Gaulle in coordinating the Free French and Allied interventions from outside France with the growing Resistance within France.

zone « libre » occupée. On ne pouvait plus que se cacher ici, à la campagne, et attendre des armes. Mais il fallait connaître des gens à la campagne.

✶

Pour la centième fois, Robert Basin se demandait : Et maintenant qu'est-ce que je vais faire ?

Il s'était posé la question toute la journée devant son tour qui ne ronflait pas aussi franc que d'habitude. Après tout, c'est pour les Boches qu'on travaille ici ou là.

Et maintenant qu'il était sorti de l'usine, il retournait la question dans sa tête, accoudé au parapet du pont. La Seine traînait. Les usines Renault, toutes cheminées dehors, malgré le bombardement de l'an passé, avançaient leurs proues, prêtes à appareiller pour un voyage qu'elles ne faisaient jamais. De l'autre côté, les collines de Sèvres montaient jusqu'à de faux bois où l'on ne se perd pas.

Et maintenant, qu'est-ce que je vais faire ?

Il tâtait dans sa poche l'ordre de se rendre à la gare de l'Est.[7] Le papier était toujours là, plié. Il eut envie de le jeter à l'eau. Et tout serait dit. On verrait bien. Il cracha dans l'eau.

De toutes les raisons qu'ils remâchaient ensemble depuis des jours sous la menace vague d'un départ auquel personne ne croyait pour soi — on croit qu'on gagnera à

7. The main station in Paris for trains going eastward.

la loterie, puisqu'on prend un billet ; on ne croit pas que le malheur sera pour soi : c'est pourquoi l'on réussit à vivre, malgré tout — rien ne restait. Il fallait qu'il les reprit une à une, en se les appliquant cette fois à lui-même.

Mais d'abord, il se sentait décidé à ne pas partir, bien décidé à ne pas partir. Ici aussi je travaille pour eux, c'est entendu, puisque toute l'Europe travaille pour eux. D'ailleurs, je travaille le moins possible, juste assez pour ne pas être mis à pied. Et sans compter toutes les pièces qui sont ratées, imperceptiblement. Du bon travail. Mais s'ils veulent nous envoyer en Allemagne, c'est qu'ils y voient leur intérêt : soit qu'ils pensent nous y faire travailler davantage, soit qu'ils espèrent, par la suite, nous utiliser militairement, soit qu'ils désirent compléter le coup de filet de 1940 et vider la France de tous les hommes susceptibles de prendre un jour les armes contre eux. Quelle qu'en soit la raison et peut-être sont-elles toutes également valables, si tel est leur intérêt, le nôtre est exactement inverse. Donc, il ne faut pas partir. Donc, il ne faut pas que je parte.

Et de nouveau, il entendit la question : « Et toi, qu'est-ce que tu feras si l'on te désigne ? »

Il vit venir Le Guirrec qui, lui aussi, avait reçu le matin son ordre de route. Il chercha à l'éviter, passa le pont. L'autre d'ailleurs ne semblait pas l'avoir aperçu : il marchait souvent comme s'il avait la mer devant lui.

— Et toi, qu'est-ce que tu feras, si l'on te désigne ?

Simone devait être rentrée, bien qu'elle fût obligée de faire chaque jour des heures supplémentaires.

Lorsqu'elle lui ouvrit la porte, elle comprit tout de suite :

— Tu pars, dit-elle.

Et il vit que son visage se tirait sous les yeux, comme lorsqu'elle était fatiguée, le soir, après sa journée de travail.

— J'ai reçu ma convocation, fit-il d'une voix neutre.

— Il ne faut pas partir, dit-elle.

Et il ne savait pas s'il ne devait pas partir parce qu'il ne fallait pas aider Hitler à asservir l'Europe, s'il ne devait pas partir parce qu'il l'aimait : tout était confondu en elle. Il savait que depuis qu'il la connaissait, il était devenu meilleur. Et s'il cherchait ce qu'il entendait par « meilleur » il s'expliquait à lui-même : plus conscient, comme s'il était personnellement responsable de tout.

Elle s'était déshabillée. Elle s'était étendue nue dans son lit. Et maintenant il allait la rejoindre. Ils n'étaient plus qu'un homme et une femme nue, de toute éternité.

— Ne pars pas, répéta-t-elle.

Elle avait les bras serrés autour de son cou, comme font les femmes. Il la laissa.

— Ne pars pas, dit-elle pour la troisième fois.

Elle s'était nichée toute petite contre lui, dans le creux de son épaule et de sa hanche.

— Comment faire ? dit-il.

— Je te cacherai, répondit-elle.

Et il est vrai qu'elle était sa maison.

— Mais où ? demanda-t-il.

Il voyait cette unique pièce avec un cabinet à côté.

— Qui saura que tu es ici ? reprit-elle. Je dirai que nous nous sommes disputés et que tu m'as quittée.

Elle se serra davantage contre lui pour éloigner le sort que, peut-être, elle faisait naître en l'évoquant.

— Mais pour ma carte d'alimentation ?

— Je m'arrangerai. Puis, je tâcherai de te cacher à la campagne. Je dirai à ma tante que tu es mon fiancé. — Et tout à coup elle regretta d'avoir jeté ce mot entre eux : il ne fallait pas qu'il se crût lié à elle. — Elle a une petite ferme au milieu des bois. Trois maisons qui sont dans les bois.

Il s'en remettait à cette femme qui était sienne, à sa parole sûre qui organisait autour de lui, tranquillement, toute la complicité d'un pays.

— Il faut que des hommes restent ici, reprit-elle, comme si elle voulait répondre à une objection qu'il ne formulait pas, l'objection de la douceur et de la lâcheté, l'objection du plus facile. Quant il faudra sortir les fusils et les mitrailleuses, alors, va, je ne te retiendrai plus.

Veillée

De l'ouest, le vent s'est levé et la lune galope en rond derrière les nuages. Les arbres, le long de la route, courbent leurs dos nus. Tout fuit et demeure.

Une porte a claqué, béant un instant sur une lumière et un feu. Et de nouveau, le village s'enfonce dans le noir, le noir « des cavernes et des marécages »,[1] plus noir encore d'être revenu. Les poteaux électriques, supportant en vain leurs ampoules mortes, montent la garde autour du palais désaffecté de la lumière. On les avait plantés juste

1. Given how Thomas juxtaposes hearth light, electricity (representing scientific progress), and the courthouse (justice) against the threatening darkness (the Nazi occupation), the likely source for the quotation is André Lefèvre's *La philosophie* (C. Reinwald, 1879), a massive history of human knowledge. In it, the phrase "des cavernes et des marécages" conjures a primitive time when humankind "ne connaissait . . . ni famille, ni societé, ni justice" (175). Lefèvre continues: "Le foyer, créateur des arts et de la civilisation, devint le centre sacré de la famille," on which society was founded (175–76). In the 1880s, Lefèvre was a better-known member of the freethinkers movement, which championed scientific knowledge as key to establishing and maintaining a democratic, egalitarian, and just society. Jennifer Hecht's *The End of the Soul: Scientific Modernity, Atheism, and Anthropology in France* (Columbia UP, 2003) includes a chapter on this little-studied movement (257–95), which would have influenced French leftist intellectuals like Thomas.

avant la guerre : la route a vu clair six mois. Et maintenant, elle fuit obscurément sous le galop de la lune, dans l'immensité de l'Europe, jusque là-bas, à l'Est, où il fait clair, parce que les villages brûlent.

Des sabots claquent, courant vers l'ouest, sur la route, au rebours du vent, des sabots paisibles, de temps de paix. Une autre porte s'est ouverte, où il fait clair et chaud.

— Bonsoir, Jean, bonsoir, Marie.

— Bonsoir, Appolonie.

— Ne fais pas de bruit, tais-toi.

Laissant ses sabots à la porte, la vieille s'est approchée sur ses chaussons, puis elle s'est accroupie tout contre l'appareil de TSF.[2]

Ils tiennent un long fil qui plonge dans un seau d'eau. Et ainsi, sous le bredouillement d'une musique ennemie, ils tentent de saisir la puissance des ondes secrètes qu'ils ont choisi de déchaîner. Ici, Londres. Ici, Moscou. Ici, Alger. Et par Alger, ici l'Amérique. Ainsi vient, en cette chambre close, murmurer le monde tout entier.

Dans ce village éloigné de tout village, perdu presqu'au milieu des bois et des collines, on pourrait croire qu'on vit dans un monde fermé et qui se suffit à lui-même ; et qu'au fond la guerre ne l'atteint pas, puisqu'elle ne change

2. German policy made owning or listening to a radio, particularly one tuned to a non-German radio station, punishable by death.

rien aux saisons. On pourrait le croire. On voudrait surtout nous le faire croire ; dans les journaux, on aime à chanter le bonheur nostalgique des champs, la sagesse ancestrale des paysans, à prêcher le « retour à la terre », source de toute richesse, de toute paix, de toute vérité. Mais ici, on sait à quoi s'en tenir, on sait que depuis des dizaines et des dizaines d'années, on est attiré vers la chance des villes, et que, quelquefois, on fait sa chance là-bas ; on est attiré vers le mouvement, et vers la lumière, et vers l'aventure des villes, comme les plantes se tournent vers la lumière, aussi irrésistiblement ; qu'ici, les maisons sont pauvres et ruinées, que le fumier monte devant les portes, que demain sera exactement comme aujourd'hui, et qu'on mourra comme on est né, sans s'être aperçu de la vie qui coule entre deux. Exactement, comme mon père et mon grand-père. Alors, à quoi cela me sert-il à moi d'être né ? C'est ailleurs, et sous d'autres formes, que la vie se joue et change. Et quant à la sagesse ? Le père Chambert a mis le feu par vengeance à la meule de son voisin qui avait refusé de lui vendre un arpent jouxte ses champs . . .

— Écoute donc, cette fois, c'est Londres.

. . . et que nous sommes solidaires de tout ce qui se passe sur la terre, même si on l'oublie un instant dans le chant d'un merle.

On se penche plus près du poste, d'où dépend notre destin, car on sait bien, ici aussi, que notre vie prendra la forme que lui imposera cette guerre.

Mais Appolonie pense à son fils qui ne reviendra plus. Son mari aussi est mort à l'autre guerre. Est-ce qu'il y aura ainsi des guerres jusqu'à la fin des siècles ? Ou est-ce qu'un jour enfin on saura faire un monde où elles n'existeront plus ? Cela ne lui rendra pas son fils, l'être unique qu'était son fils et qui ne sera jamais plus . . .

Jean a tourné un bouton et la voix est revenue.

Mais le temps de la paix est un rêve de femme. Mais le temps de la paix se conquiert, et durement. Et pour nous, ce n'est ni la paix ni la guerre, mais un temps indéterminé auquel on ne sait donner aucun nom. Son fusil est enterré au bout du jardin. Il faudra qu'il aille voir si la rouille ne le ronge pas, et le graisser. Ce n'est pas qu'il se sente de la haine. Quand il est parti pour cette guerre, il n'éprouvait aucune haine contre les hommes qui étaient tapis de l'autre côté du Rhin, comme ceux de ce côté-ci. Mais contre ce que ces hommes défendaient et étaient obligés de vouloir imposer au monde, et nous ont imposé ici, avec les complicités que l'on sait, oui, il a de la haine. Et contre ces longs jours et ces longs mois d'attente où s'énervaient les courages, ces longs jours et ces longs mois où l'on sentait sourdre l'inquiétude, s'insinuer, puis se préciser la trahison. Et pourquoi pendant ces longs mois, voyions-nous des avions allemands venir survoler les terrains d'atterrissage, quand nous venions de recevoir l'ordre de ne pas tirer ? Et pourquoi, pendant ces longs mois, ne trouva-t-on que le temps de venir, dans la forêt Frévillard, planter des jalons pour construire une ligne de défense, alors que nous étions tous inemployés ? Oui, contre tout cela, il a de la haine. Mais maintenant, il sait que son fusil est caché au bout du jardin. Et pourquoi il l'a caché. Et que d'autres, comme lui, attendent de village en village, le signal . . .

. . . Et où va-t-il ainsi la nuit, songe Marie, avec sa bicyclette, pour ne revenir qu'au matin ? Et encore parfois ne revient-il pas, mais va tout de suite à son travail. Et pourtant il m'a juré que l'histoire avec cette fille rousse était bien finie et qu'il n'a pas d'autre femme que moi. Alors où peut-il bien passer ainsi la nuit et d'où peut-il bien ne revenir qu'au matin, tout transi de brouillard et de rosée ? Et encore faut-il, moi, que je lui prépare une chemise propre, et que j'allume le feu pour qu'il se réchauffe et qu'il ait son café. Et qu'est-ce qui le ferait si ce n'était pas moi ? Et pourquoi faut-il que ce soit moi qui l'aime, qui l'aime à en perdre la raison, à l'attendre éveillée toute la nuit ?

Elle le regarde. Il est penché sur l'appareil de TSF. Elle voit son visage tendu, dont le feu de la cheminée éclaire les méplats. Et les rides de son front. Et tout son bonheur à elle, et son désespoir à elle, qui sont enclos sous ce front ; sa vie et sa mort à elle, qui sont encloses dans ce front et dans ce corps. Elle se sent n'exister que par lui et elle sait qu'en ce moment elle n'existe pas pour lui, que lui n'existe à son tour que dans le murmure lointain et brouillé de ces voix magiques : celles qui parlent actuellement, à Londres, à Moscou, à Alger . . . J'en perds la tête.

Elle voudrait s'approcher de lui, mettre son front sur ses genoux dans une supplication ardente et prosternée. Mais qu'est-ce que penserait la vieille Appolonie, si elle la voyait s'incliner ainsi devant lui, comme une esclave des anciens temps, elle qui lui dit souvent : « T'es folle, pire qu'une chatte, ma fille. Va, aucun homme ne vaut qu'on pleure pour lui. Sauf son fils, sais-tu bien. Sauf son fils ».

Maintenant, la radio s'est arrêtée. Appolonie demande :

— Raconte-moi ce qu'on a dit. Aujourd'hui, c'est le jour de ma mauvaise oreille.

Et Marie se tend aussi vers ses paroles : c'est Stalingrad que les Allemands ne prendront pas, parce que depuis des mois et des mois les Russes s'y maintiennent et que, maintenant, l'effort des assaillants est brisé. C'est Stalingrad, là-bas, à l'Est, si loin que le vent d'ici se perd en route et tombe avant que d'y arriver, Stalingrad où chaque maison est un fortin, chaque rue, une tranchée :

— Les Russes nous montrent comment il faut savoir se battre, comment il faut savoir mourir.

Qui parle de mourir ce soir ?

Appolonie a ouvert la porte. Et le vent s'est engouffré un instant, faisant vaciller la flamme de la cheminée. On entend clapoter les sabots dans la cour.

Elle, elle s'est retournée et elle pâlit jusqu'à ses paupières qui restent mauves, en le voyant décrocher sa vieille veste de cuir.

— Tu pars encore ce soir ? dit-elle.

Il a pris son air mauvais, son front barré. Il ne répond pas. Elle sait qu'il ne faut pas faire un geste pour le retenir, qu'il la repousserait.

Elle l'a entendu encore dans le hangar où il range sa bicyclette. Puis elle ne l'a plus entendu . . .

Le tilleul

Dès le début, « ils » avaient occupé « le Château ».

De sa loge, elle les voyait aller et venir. Toute la journée, c'était un vacarme de bottes, de moteurs et de chants. La première fois qu'elle les avait vu relever la sentinelle, dans cette cérémonie qu'ils font au pas de l'oie, elle avait cru mourir de rire (si elle avait eu envie de rire, mais elle n'en avait guère envie). Un jour, un jeune soldat était allé prendre son poste — un, deux, un, deux — en levant très haut et très raide la jambe, puis il était tombé au moment de tourner. Et elle avait ri toute seule de contentement — et très contente qu'ils la vissent rire. Mais un officier avait donné des coups de pied au soldat qui gisait encore. Le soldat s'était relevé, très rouge, restant là, au port d'arme, tandis que l'officier l'engueulait en une langue qu'elle ne comprenait pas. Mais on n'a pas besoin de comprendre. Et elle s'était sentie pleine de pitié. Oui, c'était une sorte de pitié pour le soldat. Puis, ceux-là étaient partis et avaient été remplacés par d'autres. Mais c'était toujours le même vacarme de bottes, de moteurs et de chants.

On n'en avait pas vu pendant quelques mois. Les gens du pays lui disaient :

« Alors ils sont partis, tes doryphores ? ».[1] Et, bien sûr, ils occupaient toujours la France, mais de n'en avoir plus chez nous, on éprouvait un incroyable allégement. La Renaude s'était décidée alors à remettre un peu d'ordre dans le château, « pour si Monsieur revenait qu'il ne voie pas ça ».

Les clous des bottes s'étaient imprimés dans les parquets, les chaises en bois de rose de la salle à manger étaient brisées. Quant aux livres de la bibliothèque, elle les avait retrouvés un matin sur la grande pelouse, devant la maison. Il avait plu et ils étaient tout tâchés. Le Renaude ne comprenait pas grand'chose aux livres, mais elle savait que Monsieur avait toujours le nez fourré dedans. Elle les avait donc ramassés pieusement et mis à l'abri dans l'autre chambre de la loge, celle où elle rangeait son miel, ses pommes et ses noix.

Elle avait bien passé un mois à ranger les vêtements dans les armoires, à nettoyer les carreaux, à recoudre les rideaux. Et cela avait pris un air de paix, lorsqu'ils étaient revenus. Elle en aurait pleuré, la Renaude, à cause de tout le mal qu'elle s'était donné pour rien.

---

1. *Doryphore* is a type of potato beetle. In the occupied zone, the French came to equate German soldiers with *doryphores* because both were so numerous and both depleted the potato supply.

Mais ils n'étaient qu'un petit groupe. Et ils avaient expliqué — il y en avait un, un petit, qui parlait assez bien français — qu'ils venaient juste pour garder le pont du chemin de fer qui franchissait la rivière au bout du parc. Et elle avait répondu : « Bon, bon », pour couper court. Elle n'allait pas entrer en conversation avec eux, n'est-ce pas ? Et elle avait rejeté sa charge d'herbe sur son dos, en geignant un peu du mouvement qu'elle faisait. Alors il lui avait dit :

— Permettez, Mâtâme.

Il avait pris la charge d'herbes et l'avait remontée jusqu'aux clapiers, à travers tout le parc.

Le lendemain, il l'avait vue qui descendait à l'herbe, avec sa faucille et sa toile. Il les lui avait prises des mains et il était allé couper l'herbe à sa place. Et chaque jour, maintenant, à la même heure, il venait chercher de lui-même la faucille et la toile, pour couper l'herbe. Il y avait aussi un grand blond qui allait puiser son seau à la fontaine. Lui, ne parlait pas du tout français. Il disait seulement « Grand'mère » — le seul mot que l'autre lui avait appris — en passant sa main sur les cheveux de la Renaude. Et c'est vrai qu'elle avait les cheveux tout blancs, et qu'elle était devenue, jour après jour, semblable à une vieille femme. C'étaient de bons gars.

Alors elle s'était demandée ce qu'elle pouvait faire pour eux. Elle les voyait raccommoder eux-mêmes leurs chaussettes. Et ça fait pitié, malgré tout, un homme qui tient une aiguille. Même quand cet homme est un ennemi, est chez vous. Et elle s'était mise à raccommoder leurs chaussettes.

Dans le village, on lui disait : « La Renaude, c'est-y que tu deviens collaboratrice ? ».

Elle s'en défendait. C'étaient de bons enfants, voilà tout. Et à vivre tout le temps ensemble, qu'est-ce que vous feriez, vous autres ? Mais non, là, elle n'aimait pas leur Hitler, ni le Maréchal, ni M. Laval.[2] Ah ! ça non, celui-là. Elle avait même déchiré le portrait du Maréchal qu'elle avait acheté au début, parce qu'on lui avait dit que c'était obligatoire d'avoir le portrait du Maréchal chez soi. Alors, vous voyez bien.

On était arrivé à l'automne, avec les brumes épaisses qui montent, le matin, de la rivière, stagnent bas jusque vers dix heures, puis brusquement éclatent pour laisser passer le soleil ; avec la nuit qui descend tôt, qui commence à exister en tant que nuit et laisse prévoir aux plus imprévoyants que l'hiver va venir bientôt.

---

2. In contrast to how they viewed Pétain, the French overwhelmingly despised Pierre Laval, who served briefly in 1940 as vice president of the Council of State before being ousted. He returned with Nazi support in April 1942 as minister of foreign affairs, information, and the interior. Like Pétain, Laval was charged with treason after the war, but unlike Pétain, Laval was executed.

Souvent Hans s'attardait, le soir, auprès d'elle. Il restait sous la lampe, auprès d'elle. Si seulement elle avait eu dix ans de moins, si seulement elle n'avait pas eu ces cheveux blancs qui la faisaient appeler « grand'mère ». A vrai dire, elle n'avait que quarante-cinq ans. Mais on lui donnait bien dix ans de plus que son âge. Et d'ailleurs, elle aurait pu être sa mère . . .

Un soir qu'il toussait, elle lui dit : « Attendez, je vais vous faire une tasse de tilleul », parce qu'elle était contente de faire quelque chose pour lui, exactement comme l'aurait fait sa mère. Elle alla chercher dans la pièce à côté, le pot de miel qu'elle gardait pour les rhumes d'hiver. Elle lui dit en lui tendant une cuillère d'argent qui datait de son mariage : « Sucrez-vous autant que vous voulez ».

Et maintenant, il léchait la cuillère, comme un enfant.

— Il y a bien longtemps que je n'ai mangé de miel, dit-il. Chez nous, en Allemagne, il n'y a que les capitalistes qui puissent se payer ça. C'est bien pire encore qu'ici, le capitalisme.

La Renaude ne savait pas très bien ce qu'on entendait par « capitalisme ». Elle savait seulement que ça existait aussi bien ici qu'en Allemagne, puisque Hans le disait.

— C'est Hitler qui a sauvé le capitalisme chez nous. Et c'est nous qui le sauvons chez vous. Hitler, voilà ce que je lui fais.

Il cracha dans la cheminée et cela grésilla. « Voila ce que je lui fais », répéta-t-il.

— Alors, je me demande pourquoi vous l'avez pris pour chef, dit la Renaude.

— Et vous, pourquoi avez-vous votre Maréchal? répondit Hans brusquement. Vous l'avez parce que vous êtes vaincus.

— Mais vous êtes vainqueurs, vous, dit la Renaude.

— Nous sommes vaincus, dit Hans. Nous sommes vaincus depuis le 30 janvier 1933.

La Renaude ne savait pas ce qui s'était passé le 30 janvier 1933.[3] Mais elle ne le demanda pas. Il continuait de parler tout seul en regardant le feu, comme s'il voyait dans le feu ce qu'il décrivait.

Et dans le feu apparaissaient les faubourgs noirs d'une grande ville, toutes les scories de maisons et d'usines qui s'amassent aux portes des grandes villes et semblent ne devoir y pénétrer jamais. Et tous ces hommes et ces femmes qui campent aux portes des grandes villes, dans de petites maisons de briques et de plâtras, qu'on tolère là à cause du service des usines ; et ces grandes casernes que la fumée rend grises, quotidiennement et irrémédiablement grises, où l'on entasse ceux qui servent les usines. Et pas de joie. Et pas de travail dans les

3. The date Hitler was named chancellor of Germany.

années qui suivirent l'autre guerre. Mais le chômage et la faim.

Lui, c'était un petit garçon. Il suivait dans les rues des cortèges avec des drapeaux rouges qui claquaient au vent et de grandes banderoles où l'on réclamait une vie que l'on pût vivre humainement. Pour Hans, c'était d'avoir du pain tous les jours, et même du beurre dessus, quelquefois, ou des confitures. Et une boite de soldats de plomb comme celle qu'il avait vue au bazar de la Friedrichstrasse. Quand on a dix ans, c'est cela, la vie plus humaine.

Mère disait : « Ce petit, il finira par attraper un mauvais coup ». Elle se retournait alors contre son mari, furieusement : « Il y a pourtant assez de toi ! » Hans se souvenait d'hommes qui venaient à la maison, tard le soir, après leur travail. Ils se penchaient, les uns près des autres, au-dessus de la table où traînaient les restes du repas. Ils parlaient bas, avec rapidité. Hans ne les comprenait pas. Son père levait la tête et disait : « Va-t-en, Hans, va dans la chambre à côté. On n'a pas besoin de toi ici ». Hans n'aimait pas la chambre à côté, où il n'y avait pas de fenêtre.

C'était un cabinet noir, pour tout dire. Il y retrouvait sa mère qui, assise sur une caisse, sanglotait : « Tout ça se terminera mal ».

On savait maintenant qu'il fallait se méfier du chef de service de la Compagnie du gaz, qui habitait quelques maisons plus loin et chez qui mère allait faire des ménages — mais père maintenant le lui interdisait —, qu'il fallait se méfier du représentant en objets ménagers du premier étage, qu'il ne fallait rien dire devant eux, parce que c'étaient des nazis : on les voyait, le dimanche, parader dans leur uniforme tout neuf. Dans les rues, les garçons commençaient à jouer « aux nazis et aux communistes ». Hans ne voulait pas être nazi.

Père revenait, le soir, plus soucieux que jamais. Il disait : « Kaufmann, Hübner, viennent d'être pris ». Mère le suppliait : « Je t'en prie, cesse. C'est tenter Dieu ». Il levait les épaules : « Ce n'est pas maintenant que je vais m'arrêter, maintenant qu'on a besoin de moi ».

Les jours passaient. Père était toujours en liberté. C'était que ni Kaufmann, ni Hübner n'avaient livré aucun nom. Peu à peu parvenaient les bruits de ce qui se passait dans les prisons, dans les camps. Les tortures . . .

Hans se tut, les yeux sur le feu. La Renaude releva ses lunettes, dit :

— Chez nous, en France, ces choses-là ne sont pas possibles.

— Ces choses-là sont possibles partout, dit Hans. Hitler trouvera des hommes parmi vous pour faire ces choses-là. Chez vous aussi, il trouvera des hommes pour faire cela, appuya-t-il.

Le feu grésilla. On entendit une chouette hululer dans le bois proche. Il faisait tout à fait nuit.

— Un jour, vers quatre heures du matin, on frappa à la porte. J'entends encore mon père : « N'ouvre pas ». C'est la dernière parole que j'ai entendu dire à mon père. Je me souviens du ton de cette parole. Mais les coups redoublèrent : « Ouvrez, police », criait-on. Puis : « Si vous n'ouvrez pas, on arrêtera aussi votre femme et votre fils ». Alors, mon père est allé à la porte, et l'a ouverte.

Les policiers fouillèrent partout. Ils ne trouvèrent rien. Ma mère pleurait dans un coin. Puis, ils emmenèrent mon père. On sut qu'il avait été fusillé quelques jours plus tard, dans une fournée.

— Mon pauvre gars, murmura la Renaude.

— Alors, ils essayèrent de nous faire croire qu'ils parlaient au nom du peuple allemand, qu'ils recherchaient le bien de la communauté allemande. Ils nous enrôlaient, nous, les jeunes, dans des camps où ils prétendaient nous dresser comme des bêtes savantes. Et il y en a beaucoup qui, à force de faire les gestes qu'on leur imposait, finissaient par penser qu'ils accomplissaient ces gestes librement, qu'ils étaient d'accord avec leurs gestes. Ma mère, parce qu'elle allait mendier des vêtements au Secours d'Hiver, finissait par croire que c'était bien, ainsi, d'être une mendiante. Moi, je me souvenais de la mort de mon père. J'avais réussi à me procurer les livres interdits qu'il lisait. J'apprenais à comprendre la mort de mon père. C'est le seul espoir qui nous reste d'être sauvés. Et à vous aussi, peut-être.

Les évadés

On voit un champ carré, coupé au cordeau, au milieu des bois de pin et de bouleaux, dont les feuilles perpétuellement tremblent, même quand il n'y a pas de vent.

On voit un grand lambeau de ciel qui va, déclinant, sur d'autres champs coupés de bois. Les bouleaux, perpétuellement, crépitent de leurs pépites d'argent dans le soleil couchant.

On voit un homme courbé en deux et désouchant la terre restée si longtemps enclavée dans le bois qu'elle en garde les racines, comme des serpents lovés en elle, ou comme une maladie.

L'homme lève sa houe, l'abat sur une racine, la dégage péniblement, la rejette. Un moment s'arrête et lève son visage en sueur. Les feuilles des bouleaux n'ont pas cessé de trembler pendant ce temps-là.

Deux hommes sont apparus au bord du bois, deux hommes déteints. Ils ont regardé autour d'eux et ils ont vu l'homme qui désouchait la terre au milieu du bois. Ils sont venus à lui.

— Salut, disent-ils.

— Salut, répond l'autre.

— Est-ce que vous connaissez une source par ici ? disent-ils. Nous n'avons pas bu depuis ce matin.

Et tout à coup, on entend chanter la source qu'on n'avait pas entendue jusque là parce qu'on est trop habitué a désoucher depuis des jours ce coin-là, pour remarquer encore les bruits qui ne changent pas.

— Par là, dit l'homme.

Ils se sont agenouillés au bord de la source. C'est un tuyau qui sort du talus et jette l'eau dans une auge de pierre. Cela a dû être fait dans les temps anciens, quand il y avait un village par ici, dont on trouve encore les vestiges. Ils ont bu d'abord dans leurs mains. Ensuite, ils ont mis leurs tètes sous le jet d'eau et ils ont bu, en même temps que l'eau lavait leurs visages souillés de poussière. Ils ont plaqué alors leurs cheveux sur leurs têtes et, malgré leurs joues mal rasées, ils ont été ce qu'ils étaient : des hommes tout jeunes encore, presque des gamins.

L'homme avait compris tout de suite ce qu'ils étaient ; c'était par ici que passait la route des pèlerinages, c'est par ici que passe la route des évadés.

— Et maintenant, disent-ils, où est-ce que nous pourrons coucher ce soir ?

Sur la terre déclive, l'homme a montré un toit qui fumait et, serrés autour, les toits des granges et des étables.

— Est-ce que ce sont de bons Français ? demandent-ils.

— Oui, ce sont de bons Français. Vous direz que vous venez de la part de Martin, que vous avez trouvé désouchant là-haut.

Ils sont partis en traînant leurs gros souliers. De temps en temps, une pierre heurtée roule sur le sentier et s'éboule.

Les feuilles des bouleaux se sont remises à trembler.

Le chien tire sur sa chaîne et aboie. Les poules enquêtent autour du fumier. Ils ont été droit à la porte, dont le haut seul est ouvert. Ils ont frappé. Une femme est venue, toute jeune, avec des cheveux frisés : c'est peut-être la première femme française qu'ils voient depuis longtemps. Ils ont demandé :

— Est-ce que nous pourrons coucher dans la grange ?

Elle leur a dit :

— Je vous ferai deux lits dans la chambre à grain. On n'a pas encore battu et il y a de la place.

Car maintenant, on sait que ce ne sont pas des trimards, de ces gens sans feu ni lieu qui faisaient comme s'ils cherchaient du travail, mais n'en voulaient pas trouver et s'enfuyaient quand on leur disait : « Restez, on vous donnera bien de l'ouvrage ». Maintenant, tout le monde peut devenir trimard, d'un jour à l'autre. Et mon frère qui est prisonnier, et nous demain, si une bombe tombe sur la ferme, ou qu'on reparte, comme à l'exode.[1] Mais moi, cette fois, je ne repartirai pas. J'aime mieux mourir ici.

Et maintenant, autour de la table brune, ils mangent un vrai repas, le premier depuis des années. Oui, cela fait maintenant des années qu'on n'a mangé une omelette, et du lard, et de ce pain-là.

Un à un, ils sont revenus des champs : le Patron, et l'Homme de cour, et Joseph le Charretier, et même Martin qui est toujours en retard, comme s'il ne pouvait pas se séparer de quelque chose qui le retient là-haut, on ne sait quoi, car il n'y a rien de beau là-haut, sinon les feuilles des bouleaux.

Viennent les marches des premiers jours : ceux qui tombaient, de fatigue, on les relevait à coups de crosse, jusqu'à ce qu'ils tombassent de nouveau, épuisés. Il y en a un qui est mort comme cela, tout à côté de moi. Je n'ai rien pu faire pour lui.

Viennent la longueur des jours et la lenteur et la torpeur des camps. On attendait la nourriture ; on attendait les lettres ; on attendait les paquets ; on attendait que le jour fût passé ; on attendait des nouvelles qui n'arrivaient

1. This "*exode*" refers to the mass movement of populations—some two million from Belgium, Luxembourg, and Holland, another two million from northern France, and two million more from Paris—toward the south of France in May and June 1940, where they sought safety from the invading German army.

jamais ; et il fallait se lever quand même, le lendemain matin, bien qu'il fût certain que le jour ne leur apporterait que l'attente.

Puis on les fit monter dans un train. A travers les fenêtres grillagées du wagon à bestiaux, ils voyaient glisser une grande terre déserte, une plaine qui n'en finissait pas de s'étaler, avec des plaques de neige ici et là, bien qu'on fût à la fin d'avril, et des genévriers tordus, une grande terre triste avec un ciel gris et sans fin par dessus. Puis la plaine s'arrêta à une gare et ils virent une femme qui leur faisait des signes à sa fenêtre. Elle disparut un moment et revint portant un grand carton sur lequel était écrit en grosses lettres : « Français, vous êtes ici en Pologne, nous ferons ce que nous pourrons pour vous aider ». Puis la femme disparut et la plaine se remit à glisser. C'était comme s'ils ne devaient plus s'arrêter de rouler sur la terre : toujours plus loin vers l'Est, toujours plus loin.

Pendant des mois et des mois, ils travaillèrent à des fortifications. Mais le soir, quand ils revenaient au camp, courbatus et recrus, des enfants se glissaient jusqu'à eux, sur la route, et leur apportaient quelque nourriture, bien qu'ils eussent eux-mêmes fort peu à manger. Ainsi ils tenaient la promesse de bienvenue de la femme. Ainsi des mois. Et c'est alors qu'ils s'étaient rencontrés tous deux et qu'ils s'étaient promis de ne plus se quitter.

Le robinet de l'évier s'égouttait. Il n'y avait dehors aucun bruit. Mais ici venaient déferler les images de l'Europe en guerre et de sa souffrance.

— En Allemagne, nous avons travaillé en usine. Il nous était interdit de parler aux civils allemands. Mais le contremaître, sous prétexte de nous expliquer notre travail, venait chaque jour nous donner les nouvelles de la radio anglaise, tu te souviens, Jean. Il disait : « Quand vous rentrerez en France, vous direz bien que nous ne sommes pas tous derrière Hitler. Vous direz bien . . . » Tu te souviens, Jean.

Et maintenant, ils se devaient de répéter ce que le contremaître allemand les avait chargés de dire. Religieusement. Les autres, Martin et Joseph, et le Patron, hochaient la tête : alors, pourquoi la guerre durait-elle si longtemps, s'ils avaient assez de leur Hitler ?

On entendit la sonnerie du téléphone. La femme se leva et revint toute pâle :

— C'est des Charmettes qu'on téléphone, dit-elle. Ils ont eu la visite des gendarmes, à cause de ce bœuf dont on a retrouvé la peau enterrée dans la forêt . . . Les gendarmes sont en route. Ils viennent ici.[2]

2. The mention of an ox hide implies that the police are looking for poachers.

On leur fit traverser la cour. La lune se levait, éclairant la mare. Dans les hauts, un rossignol chantait. On les poussa dans une petite grange qui sentait le foin sec.

— On viendra vous chercher, le danger passé, dit le Patron.

Et l'on referma la porte derrière eux.

Ils étaient couchés dans le foin, côte à côte, comme depuis tant de mois. Ils n'avaient pas peur; il leur semblait que rien ne pouvait plus leur arriver. Demain, ils seraient chez eux. L'aventure s'achevait.

— Qui sait si nous ne regretterons pas ce temps ? dit l'un d'eux.

Cette phrase-là, il n'aurait pas osé la prononcer plus tôt. Et maintenant encore, elle sonnait comme un sacrilège. Et l'autre répondit — dans le noir, ils ne se voyaient pas — :

— Serons-nous jamais capables de nous réintroduire dans la vie ?

Et tout à coup, il songea avec une ineffable tendresse et un indicible écœurement au coin de salon, où sa mère tricotait devant une tasse de thé, qu'elle achevait à petits coups. Quelque chose était fini pour lui : le temps qui avait été avant, le garçon qu'il avait été avant. Et il ne connaissait pas encore l'autre qui était né depuis.

Le rossignol chanta plus haut.

Sa mère ouvrit les yeux, sourit à peine. Son visage de morte redevint un instant un visage de vivante. Puis, elle referma les yeux. Mais du fond de son néant, elle lui avait fait signe qu'elle était encore vivante, qu'elle vivrait.

Anne eut envie de se jeter au pied du lit, de remercier quelqu'un, quelque chose, Dieu. Mais si elle devait remercier Dieu de la résurrection de sa mère, de cet événement personnellement heureux qui venait de lui arriver, il fallait aussi attribuer à Dieu ce monde atroce où l'on vivait, ces cataclysmes individuels qui constituaient à chaque instant le cataclysme commun, toute la souffrance et le misérable bonheur de la terre. Il n'y avait, au-dessus des hommes, personne à qui elle pût rendre grâce de sa joie, sans le tenir aussi responsable de la souffrance. Si un tel être avait existé et fût doué de conscience et de raison, ce ne pouvait être qu'un monstre capricieux et puéril : cela n'expliquait rien, de lui attribuer l'accident du Bien et le décharger du Mal en déclarant ses voies insondables. L'existence du Mal suffisait à la négation de Dieu, et la négation de Dieu était sa seule excuse. Elle croyait bien que ces problèmes porte-à-faux ne se posaient plus pour elle depuis longtemps. Mais voilà qu'à cause de ce bonheur — ce bonheur dont on n'a pas l'habitude — ils réapparaissaient. La conscience, comme la terre, est formée de couches géologiques d'âges différents.

Elle s'assit à côté du lit de sa mère, lui prit la main sans la bouger, comme si elle craignait d'effaroucher cette vie unique et qui revenait. Elle sentait la peau tiède, et souple, et vivante de la main sous la sienne. Elle en baisa le mince poignet veiné.

« Ma pauvre maman », murmura-t-elle. Et des larmes de grâce lui vinrent aux yeux.

Le chirurgien entra.

— Elle a ouvert les yeux, dit Anne.

Il sourit :

— Je vous avais affirmé que je la sauverais.

Rien de mauvais ne pouvait venir de cet homme-là. Elle se sentait près de lui pleine de confiance en la science de cet homme. En l'homme. Elle songea brusquement à tous ces jeunes hommes qui mouraient *actuellement.* Tout était absurde.

Elle demeura ainsi un long moment, tenant la main de sa mère dans la sienne. Le jour glissait sur les murs blancs de la chambre de clinique. Au déplacement de l'index de soleil, elle savait que le temps passait. Tout à l'heure, il lui faudrait reprendre sa tâche. C'était un moment de répit qui lui était accordé.

Tout à coup, elle entendit des pas dans le couloir, des pas lourds et comme bottés, et qui passaient et qui passaient, sans s'arrêter nulle part. La chambre de sa mère était la dernière au fond du couloir. Les pas bottés approchaient. Elle *savait* maintenant que les pas bottés venaient pour elle. Est-ce qu'elle avait peur ? Avoir peur, c'est consentir à sa peur, ce n'est pas la ressentir. Elle avait toujours été de celles à qui il est plus facile de refuser que de s'abandonner, de se révolter que d'accepter. C'est maintenant seulement qu'elle allait savoir réellement ce qu'elle valait.

La porte s'ouvrit sans qu'on frappât. Elle *savait* ce qui serait derrière la porte : deux Allemands en uniforme s'y trouvaient. Derrière eux, le visage de l'infirmière, Mlle Benizat, apparut, livide sous son voile. Anne vit qu'un de ses yeux titillait dans l'arcade sourcilière agrandie. J'ai tout mon sang-froid, se dit-elle, puisque je suis encore capable de remarquer un détail insignifiant. J'ai tout mon sang-froid. Mais ses jambes étaient molles. Je me demande si je pourrais marcher.

— Anne Roger, demanda l'un des Allemands, avec un fort accent.

— Oui, dit-elle, en se levant. Ses jambes étaient molles, mais pouvaient pourtant la soutenir. Maintenant elle était debout devant eux — très petite devant eux — mais prête à leur tenir tête : c'est plus facile debout qu'assis.

— Veuillez nous suivre, dirent-ils.

Ils étaient d'une parfaite correction. Ni leur politesse, ni leurs menaces ne devaient avoir d'action sur elle. Elle entrait dans un monde inconnu, le monde de la bête chassée et du chasseur, où toutes les feintes, tous les pièges sont bons.

— Où ? demanda-t-elle.

— Chez vous, dirent-ils.

Elle se retourna et vit les yeux démesurément ouverts de sa mère qui la regardaient, et vit la tête de sa mère soulevée sur l'oreiller par une tension démesurée de son cou maigre. Ses lèvres tremblaient.

— Laissez-moi du moins embrasser ma mère.

Elle se pencha et posa sa bouche sur son front froid et en sueur.

— Sois tranquille, dit-elle à haute voix, il n'y a rien du tout à la maison. Je vais revenir tout à l'heure. Mlle Benizat, ajouta-t-elle, voulez-vous avoir la gentillesse de me faire préparer, pour ce soir, un lit dans la chambre de maman.

Puis elle sortit avec eux. Ce n'était pas difficile de marcher, de traverser le palier où apparaissaient furtivement des femmes de chambre, des infirmières, l'assistant. Elle les salua.

Ce n'était pas difficile de descendre l'escalier, ni de monter dans la voiture qui les attendait. Il y avait des mois qu'elle n'était montée en auto. Sur le trottoir, deux pigeons picoraient. Anne remarqua en un instant tous les gris de leurs plumes : gris-souris, gris-ardoise, gris de ciel, gris-fumée, et un gris tirant sur le roux, comme certains toits de vieilles tuiles, au soleil.

C'est peut-être la dernière fois que je vois des pigeons, se dit-elle. Alors, elle songea à sa mère et sentit son cœur devenir trop gros pour sa poitrine. Pourvu que je ne pleure pas. Il ne manquerait plus que cela. Jusque-là, elle s'était assez bien tenue, mais cela ne faisait que commencer.

La bonne vint ouvrir.

— Ah ! Mademoiselle, s'écria-t-elle, comment va ? . . .

Mais Anne vit son visage se raidir de terreur.

Ils étaient entrés. Ils avaient demandé où était son bureau et elle les avait menés à sa chambre. Et maintenant elle les voyait ouvrir tous les tiroirs, en jeter le contenu sur le tapis. De temps en temps, ils butaient sur un papier, le lisaient attentivement, le rejetaient parmi les autres. Elle, elle savait qu'ils ne pouvaient rien trouver, qu'ils pourraient retourner tout l'appartement, qu'ils ne trouveraient rien de ce qu'ils cherchaient. Maintenant elle se sentait sûre d'elle-même, elle sentait que, pas plus que son appartement, elle ne laisserait rien échapper ; elle était redevenue celle de tous les jours, pure et froide, d'une froideur passionnée.

Puis ce fut le tour des livres de la bibliothèque. Ils constatèrent : « Vous avez des morceaux choisis de Karl Marx ».

— J'ai Nietzsche, j'ai Platon, j'ai Kierkegaard, répondit-elle.

Ils secouaient les livres ouverts, puis les jetaient à terre avec ses bas et ses robes. Depuis deux heures, ils travaillaient rudement. C'étaient des hommes consciencieux et qui faisaient consciencieusement leur métier.

— Quand il faudra remettre tout ça en place ! grommela la bonne, qui, de temps en temps, venait jeter un coup d'oeil.

Anne jugea la réflexion comique. Puis elle chercha pourquoi, et découvrit que l'élément de comique venait de la disproportion entre les conséquences que la bonne envisageait et celles qui existeraient réellement. Décidément, la machine fonctionnait.

Les Allemands enfin cessèrent de fouiller. Ils revinrent dans le salon, lui dirent de s'asseoir, s'assirent. Je ne suis plus chez moi. C'est eux qui se sont installés chez eux. Elle entra dans le jeu, s'assit sagement comme en visite. Maintenant ce n'était plus aux choses de répondre par leur mutisme, mais à elle-même. Elle avait su organiser le silence des choses autour d'elle. Le saurait-elle garder aussi bien ? Ils commencèrent à l'interroger.

Connaissait-elle Z, professeur à . . . ? Oui, elle le connaissait. C'était un vieil ami de son père. Eh bien ! Il venait d'être arrêté. Il avait avoué.

— Avoué quoi ? demanda-t-elle. Je ne comprends pas ce que vous voulez dire.

Mais que Z fût arrêté lui portait un coup terrible. Pour lui d'abord. Pour d'autres ensuite. Pour elle-même. Il tiendra, se dit-elle. Et comme un boxeur qui a l'habitude de recevoir des coups et de les surmonter, elle se sentit dominer tout. Passa outre.

Elle se voyait assise sur cette chaise et répondre comme si elle avait été à la fois sur la scène et dans la salle. Cela a du bon, pensa-t-elle, d'avoir toujours « joué un rôle » dans la vie, de s'être efforcée de le bien jouer, de n'avoir jamais toléré en soi que ce qui convenait à ce rôle, de s'être efforcée enfin de ressembler à celle qu'on a choisi d'être, et ainsi, peu à peu, de le devenir : ne pas donner prise à son propre mépris.

Elle s'entendait nier, nier, nier, comme la défense la plus facile (celle qui convenait le mieux à sa sincérité, car il y a une certaine façon d'être sincère, à l'intérieur du rôle). Non, elle n'avait pas d'activité politique. Non, elle ne s'occupait de rien. Non, elle ne savait pas ce qu'ils voulaient dire. Non, elle n'avait jamais entendu parler de celle conspiration, de ces réunions, de ces tracts.

Le visage de celui qui l'interrogeait lui semblait démesurément grossi derrière la table. Elle voyait les rides de sa peau rougeâtre et les pores larges aux ailes du nez et aux joues. Ses yeux n'avaient pas de regard : c'étaient des globes verts striés de veinules plus foncées, sans plus d'expression que deux billes d'aigue-marine. Non. Non. Non. L'autre avait un long menton glabre qui pendait et qu'il retenait dans sa main comme s'il craignait de le perdre. Et en même temps elle s'entendait faire la bête et la naïve : dire non.

— Très bien, dit l'homme au menton glabre qui, jusqu'ici n'avait pas prononcé un mot. Nous aurons d'autres moyens de vous faire parler.

— Veuillez nous suivre, ajouta-t-il poliment.

Ce fut le souvenir de sa mère qui revint, de ses pauvres yeux agrandis dans son visage maigre, de ce poignet bleuté au bout de ce bras réduit. Jamais je ne la reverrai. Sa gorge se serra. Etait-ce la peur ? Etait-ce la peine ? Elle avait choisi de tout refuser.

— Puis-je dire un mot à la bonne ? demanda-t-elle.

— Devant nous, dirent-ils.

Marielle était assise sur le tabouret de la cuisine. Quand ils entrèrent, elle se mit à trembler si fort qu'on entendait claquer ses dents.

— Mariette, dit Anne, voulez-vous aller tout de suite à la clinique prévenir maman : qu'elle ne s'inquiète pas. Ces

Messieurs me relâcheront dès qu'ils auront reconnu leur méprise.

Elle l'embrassa. C'est peut-être la dernière fois que j'embrasse quelqu'un.

Puis ses talons sonnèrent dans l'entrée, aussi durement que leurs bottes.

FTP

Franceis i unt ferut de cor et de vigur.

—*La Chanson de Roland*

On est venu le prévenir: « Un train d'Allemands passera ce soir à vingt-trois heures trente-quatre ».[1]

Entre la gare et la forêt, il y a cinq minutes à peine. Donc, le train allemand passera à onze heures trente-neuf. Pourtant, il s'est rendu au petit bistrot, près de la gare, où René déjeune d'ordinaire. René, dans un coin de la salle, mangeait avec le chef de gare. Il s'est approché de la table. Ils se sont dit bonjour d'un air négligent et ils ont parlé de la pluie et du beau temps.

1. The Francs-Tireurs et Partisans (FTP) was a resistance group established in 1941 as the military branch of the French Communist Party (but was open to non-Communists). The fact that Thomas footnotes the title of this story in the first edition of *Contes d'Auxois* suggests the group was still unfamiliar to readers when she wrote the story. The FTP would soon, however, count among France's most important resistance groups and would owe its growing reputation to its strategy of coordinating small, anonymous groups, both urban and rural, to sabotage railways and factories serving Nazi interests, to fire on German soldiers, and to punish collaborators. Its increasing effectiveness is borne out by the fact that by fall 1943, Germany deployed troops charged with annihilating the FTP. By 1944, de Gaulle had to reckon with the FTP as a paramilitary force crucial to France's liberation from within; in February of that year, when he called for French resistance groups to unite as the Forces Françaises de l'Intérieur, the FTP agreed.

René lui a dit : « Tu ne manges pas ici ? Il y a du lapin aux pommes de terre. Il est fameux ». Il a répondu : « Non, ma femme m'attend. Elle va m'attraper si je suis en retard ». Alors, René s'est levé et lui a dit : « Je t'accompagne un bout. Je viendrai prendre mon café tout à l'heure », a-t-il crié au chef de gare.

Puis, ils sont sortis du même air négligent en allumant une cigarette sur le pas de la porte.

Ils ont fait quelques pas, tourné par une petite rue. L'herbe pousse entre les pavés. De temps en temps, une vieille soulève un rideau et le laisse retomber. Ce sont des visages qu'on connaît, qui font partie de la rue. C'est René qui travaille à la gare et c'est Paul, le commis de banque, des copains de toujours. Ils ont fait leur service militaire ensemble et ils ont été faits prisonniers ensemble pendant cette « drôle de guerre ».[2] Mais ils ont réussi à s'évader, avant qu'on ne les envoie en Allemagne. Et la mère de Paul, je la connais : nous allions à l'école ensemble. Il a épousé une institutrice, une petite brune de Paris, un peu fière, meilleure qu'on ne croit. René, lui,

---

2. The *drôle de guerre*, known in English as the phony war, began on 3 September 1939, when France and Britain declared war on Nazi Germany, and ended on 10 May 1940, when Germany invaded Belgium, Luxembourg, Holland, and France. Between these dates, French and British troops waited behind the Maginot Line to face German troops but launched no significant offensives.

est encore garçon. C'est dommage qu'il ne se marie pas : il pourrait rendre une femme heureuse. C'est Paul qui rentre chez lui : il habite au bout de la rue, presqu'aux champs, une maison d'un étage, avec un jardin à fleurs devant, mais il y a planté des pommes de terre et des épinards.

On a laissé retomber le rideau : il ne se passe jamais rien dans cette rue, qui vaille la peine de regarder. Ce n'est pas comme si j'habitais la Grand'Place avec tout le mouvement du marché et la Kommandantur qui s'est installée à la mairie ; ou même rue de la République, qu'on appelle maintenant rue du Maréchal-Pétain.

Paul rentre chez lui et René l'accompagne, parce que ce sont deux copains de toujours, voilà tout.

Paul a demandé : « Est-ce exact qu'un train d'Allemands passe ce soir à 23 heures 34. Tu as vérifié ? »

— Oui, dit René, j'ai vérifié.

— A quelle heure le dernier avant ? demanda Paul.

— C'est le train de marchandises, il passe à vingt-deux heures. Il ne s'arrête pas.

— Cinq minutes de la gare à la forêt, calcule Paul, ça fait dix heures cinq. Il faut dix bonnes minutes pour aller de Pierre Levée à la voie ferrée. Donc, il faut être à Pierre Levée à dix heures moins cinq. Toi, tu viendras directement, pour t'assurer que le train de marchandises est bien passé. Tu te charges de prévenir Louis et Alain. Moi, je préviens Paul-le-Grand (parce qu'il est beaucoup plus grand que Paul et Robert).

Ils se sont arrêtés pour rallumer une cigarette. « Moi, je fume un mélange de tabac et de barbe de maïs », parce que quelqu'un s'approchait, l'agent voyer, qu'ils saluèrent.

— Entendu, a dit René.

— Entendu, a dit Paul.

Et Paul a poussé le portillon du jardin, dont la cloche résonne dans la ruelle déserte. Puis, on a entendu ses pas sur le gravier de l'allée.

C'est Paul qui rentre chez lui pour déjeuner, tandis que René s'en retourne vers la gare : « Ce garçon-là, il faudrait lui trouver une femme, Mme Gentillon. C'est moi qui vous le dis ».

*

Et maintenant, il dit à Alice :

— Il faut que tu préviennes cet après-midi Paul-le-Grand et Robert : ce soir, dix heures moins cinq, Pierre Levée.

Elle a légèrement pâli : simplement, sa peau mate devient bistre. Elle ne demande rien. Elle attend.

— Tu leur diras de ne pas oublier leurs « carnets ».

Elle sait ce que signifient leurs « carnets ». Mais le sang est revenu sous ses joues. Elle ne dit rien. Elle attend. Il ajoute :

— C'est pour un train.

Puis elle a jeté son manteau sur ses épaules et elle est partie pour l'école.

★

Elle fait la classe du certificat d'études. Et elle pense bien que quinze de ses élèves au moins seront reçues à coup sûr. Elle s'applique à ce que rien de son trouble n'apparaisse, ne soit imperceptiblement senti. Puis, elle est allée chercher un livre dans la bibliothèque de l'école. C'est *La Chanson de Roland*. Elle y a glissé un mot. A quatre heures, elle a retenu quelques minutes Marie-Catherine, qui est la meilleure élève de la classe. Elle lui a dit : « Tiens, Marie-Catherine, tu donneras ce livre à ton père, il me l'a demandé. N'oublie pas, Marie-Catherine. »

Mais elle sait que Marie-Catherine n'oublie rien. En revenant, elle s'est arrêtée chez le cordonnier. Il y avait du monde dans la boutique. Elle a demandé :

— Quand est-ce que je pourrai vous apporter mes souliers de bois à réparer ? Voilà que la semelle s'en est encore cassée.[3]

3. Beginning in 1940, France was charged with providing six million pairs of shoes to Germany. French citizens could not purchase new shoes without a provisions card coupon (which was virtually impossible to acquire), and shoe production and repairs for the French were done with wood or paper since all available leather was used for the shoes sent to Germany. Even in peacetime, however, shoes with wooden heels were the norm for poor French schoolchildren in the countryside.

— C'est de la camelote, tout ça, a répondu Paul-le-Grand.

— Et puis, il faudrait m'enlever tout de suite un clou à ce soulier-là. Il me blesse.

Elle s'est assise sur une chaise basse et s'est mise à se déchausser. Pendant ce temps, les gens sont partis. Elle a dit très vite :

— Ce soir, dix heures moins cinq, à Pierre Levée. Tu n'oublieras pas ton carnet.

Puis, elle a remis son soulier.

Il a souri de toutes les rides de son visage, qui se plisse autour de sa bouche et autour de ses yeux. C'est un homme d'une cinquantaine d'années, solide, mais tout ridé. De nouveau, on est entré dans la boutique.

— Alors, quand est-ce que je pourrai vous apporter mes souliers de bois ?

— Pas avant la semaine prochaine, a-t-il répondu, je suis surchargé de travail.

*

Ils ont dîné. Ils ont écouté la radio. Lui, affecte d'être tranquille. Mais elle sent son inquiétude. Non : ce n'est pas de l'inquiétude, c'est de l'intérêt, un intérêt extrême à tout. Mais pour elle, c'est de l'inquiétude. Elle le regarde en essuyant la vaisselle et se dit : « Et si c'était la dernière fois que je le regarde ». Et sent son cœur. Elle n'était pas faite pour être la femme d'un héros. Elle n'était pas faite pour tendre un bouclier à son mari ou à son fils, en lui disant : « Reviens dessus ou dessous ».[4] Elle était faite pour le quotidien et la paix des jours : les leçons de lecture et d'écriture, les dictées, les problèmes de robinets ; et le soir, rentrant chez soi, pour faire le ménage et la cuisine ; et avoir un enfant et le bercer ; et avoir un mari qu'on aime, et l'aimer jusqu'à la fin.

Et au fond, qu'est-ce qui lui manquait pour accomplir ce bonheur-là ? Mais elle sait que ce bonheur-là n'est pas possible, qu'il faudrait oublier tout le reste et que chaque instant nous rappelle qu'il n'y a pas de bonheur, même le plus simple, même le plus humble, *actuellement* sans mensonge et sans égoïsme. Alors tant pis : le bonheur sera pour demain, et pour d'autres peut-être. Mais pas pour nous, pour demain.

Il faut qu'il s'en aille, s'il ne veut pas être en retard. Et il ne faut pas qu'il soit en retard. Mais Paul ne sait jamais l'heure.

— Il va être dix heures moins le quart, dit-elle.

---

4. An expression often attributed to Plutarch's *Moralia* (vol. 3, Loeb Classical Library, Harvard UP, 1931), "Come back with your shield, or on it" is what Spartan mothers are supposed to have said to their sons as they saw them off to war (241).

Il l'a embrassée distraitement. Et pourtant si c'était la dernière fois, songe-t-elle. Elle a entendu son pas sur le gravier de l'allée. Mais la sonnette du portillon ne sonne pas. Elle la décroche le soir venu, de sorte qu'on ne peut savoir si l'on sort ou si l'on rentre, la nuit. Au matin, de bonne heure, tout est remis en ordre.

*

Elle a pris son tricot et ses mains vont vite. Puis ses mains retombent sur ses genoux et il n'y a plus pour elle que l'attente et l'angoisse de l'attente.

*

Il n'y a pas de lune, mais des étoiles. Une chaude nuit qui fait déjà pressentir celles de l'été. Une belle nuit, et qu'est-ce qu'on est dessous ?

Il faut d'abord sortir de la ville. C'est facile : à cette heure on ne rencontre plus personne. Et d'ailleurs, s'il rencontrait quelqu'un, il dirait qu'il est allé fumer une cigarette dehors, par cette belle nuit, avant de se coucher. Et d'ailleurs, ses papiers sont en règle : il est un bon employé, précis, qui fait son travail, et bien connu de la ville. Qu'est-ce que cela a d'extraordinaire qu'il aille fumer une cigarette dehors, par cette belle nuit ?

Il a pris une ruelle qui longe le mur de l'usine à gaz. Après des palissades, commencent les champs et ses pieds enfoncent dans la terre molle.

Pierre Levée, c'est un carrefour de sentiers où il y a un gros hêtre et point de pierre du tout. Sans doute y avait-il là, jadis, un menhir,[5] ou quelque chose de ce genre, comme l'expliquerait Alice qui connait toutes ces vieilles histoires, tous ces vieux noms. Il songe à Alice, à tout ce qu'il a acquis depuis qu'elle est sa femme. Et si elle n'était pas sa femme, peut-être n'aurait-il pas le courage et la foi d'être ici ce soir : un homme.

Une ombre, deux ombres, sont collées aux arbres du carrefour. Il s'en approche : voilà Paul-le-Grand, voilà Alain. Voilà Louis, puis Robert.

— René nous attend là-bas. Vous avez les mitraillettes ? Vous avez les tire-fonds ?

Ils font : « Oui, oui », de l'un à l'autre.

Et pourquoi sont-ils là, ce soir, les six gars, au lieu d'être assoupis dans le repos morne de la petite ville ?

Voilà Paul-le-Grand qui marche en tête. Il a cru jadis à la transformation paisible de la terre, à la disparition de

---

5. *Menhir* is formed from the Breton words *maen*, meaning "stone," and *hir*, meaning "long." A menhir is a very large stone that stands alone or in alignment with other stones. Believed to date back as far as six to seven thousand years and distributed throughout Western Europe, menhirs are particularly concentrated in northwestern France and resonate especially with Breton culture, folklore, and history. Single menhirs, often strikingly tall, may have marked important sites or passageways for certain rituals and, later on, routes for religious pilgrimages, or *pardons*, as they are known in Brittany.

l'injustice, à l'abondance, à la paix, à la joie ; qu'on n'avait qu'à étendre la main et parler de la justice ; et que les riches se démettraient de leurs richesses et les partageraient. Et puis, peu à peu, il a appris que l'on ne gagne que par l'effort. Et c'est pourquoi il est maintenant avec ceux qui savent ce qu'ils veulent et veulent les moyens de ce qu'ils veulent.

Voilà Paul à qui sa femme, Alice, a appris que la volonté de l'homme fait l'histoire et que cette volonté de libération se poursuit, aujourd'hui comme jadis, à travers l'histoire de chaque jour, et que l'histoire n'est pas une chose qu'on subit, mais qu'on accomplit.

Et voilà Robert qui est ici, parce qu'il n'admet pas que son pays soit vaincu et ne fasse rien pour retrouver son indépendance. Et c'est pourquoi il est du côté de ceux qui, cessant d'attendre le secours d'ailleurs, luttent dès maintenant pour la libération de son pays.

Et voilà Louis, ouvrier tanneur, qui est ici pour être avec les ouvriers et les paysans de l'URSS qui ont atteint à leur libération et savent ce qu'ils défendent et pourquoi ils meurent.

Et voilà Alain, qui n'a pas dix-sept ans, parce qu'il aime à être du côté où l'on se bat, parce qu'il aime les coups — en donner et au besoin en recevoir — parce qu'il aime le courage, sans qu'il en sache même le nom.

Et voilà René qui marche au loin, seul, le long de la voie ferrée, à leur rencontre. René qui est un enfant de l'Assistance publique et qui n'a jamais connu ses parents. Il sait combien ce monde est dur à ceux qui n'ont pas de parents, et que travailler dans une gare c'est déjà pour lui une belle réussite : « Vous voyez bien que n'importe qui peut arriver à n'importe quoi, dans notre société ». Mais il sait bien, lui, que c'est un mensonge et qu'il y a, au départ, un terrible handicap qui détermine tout l'avenir, et qu'il faut que cet avenir soit déterminé enfin dans la justice.

Et ainsi ces six hommes marchent silencieusement sur la terre déserte, sous le ciel nu. Et parce que ces six hommes sont là ensemble, dans un acte de volonté et de liberté, il y a quelque chose de changé à l'histoire des hommes, quelque chose de changé dans l'Europe martelée à coups de bottes, dans l'Europe sanglante, sans visage et sans voix.

Et parce que ces six hommes sont là, et d'autres comme eux en France, et dans les autres pays d'Europe, des hommes qui ne veulent pas s'incliner, des hommes qui refusent d'être dupes, des hommes qui s'engagent tout entiers, il y a quelque chose de changé, un pas de fait, qui éloigne l'homme de l'abîme et le rapproche de l'Homme qu'ils ne sont pas encore, mais qui sera demain.

Ils sont arrivés à la grand'route qui coupe la forêt. Ils se sont arrêtés un instant, écoutant les bruits. Des grenouilles coassent. Puis le vent passe et les branches, sans feuille encore, s'agitent. Ce grincement, c'est un pin qui gémit contre un autre.

Au-dessous des bruits du ciel et de la forêt, ils essaient de percevoir le bruit des hommes : le pas d'une patrouille, le grignotement imperceptible d'une bicyclette, le lointain ronflement d'une auto. Mais rien.

Alors, rapidement, ils ont traversé la route et se sont retrouvés de l'autre côté, à l'abri des arbres. Encore quelques mètres, et c'est la voie ferrée. Une ombre agenouillée déjà y travaille. Ils sont descendus sur le ballast. Et maintenant, accroupis ou courbés le long des rails, ils ressemblent à d'étranges gnomes qu'éclairent bizarrement leurs lampes électriques.

Paul regarde sa montre :

— Est-ce fini ? demande-t-il.

Ils répondent dans un chuchotement : « Oui, c'est fini ».

Alors, ils se sont retrouvés sous les arbres, leurs mitraillettes à côté d'eux.

On a entendu au loin venir le train qui, depuis la gare, ne cesse de prendre de la vitesse : encore quelques instants, et il sera ici.

On a vu la locomotive s'incliner sur le côté et le tender la suivre dans un écroulement de ferraille. Les autres wagons sont restés sur la voie. Ou a vu les Allemands épouvantés sortir des wagons.

Alors, tranquillement, les six se sont mis à tirer. Sans plus de haine qu'un chirurgien.

Sans plus de haine.